The
Animal Ark®
Ocean Special

Lucy Daniels

*Hodder
Children's
Books*

a division of Hodder Headline Limited

Animal Ark series

1 Kittens in the Kitchen
2 Pony in the Porch
3 Puppies in the Pantry
4 Goat in the Garden
5 Hedgehogs in the Hall
6 Badger in the Basement
7 Cub in the Cupboard
8 Piglet in a Playpen
9 Owl in the Office
10 Lamb in the Laundry
11 Bunnies in the Bathroom
12 Donkey on the Doorstep
13 Hamster in a Hamper
14 Goose on the Loose
15 Calf in the Cottage
16 Koalas in a Crisis
17 Wombat in the Wild
18 Roo on the Rock
19 Squirrels in the School
20 Guinea-pig in the Garage
21 Fawn in the Forest
22 Shetland in the Shed
23 Swan in the Swim
24 Lion by the Lake
25 Elephants in the East
26 Monkeys on the Mountain
27 Dog at the Door
28 Foals in the Field
29 Sheep at the Show

30 Racoons on the Roof
31 Dolphin in the Deep
32 Bears in the Barn
33 Otter in the Outhouse
34 Whale in the Waves
35 Hound at the Hospital
36 Rabbits on the Run
37 Horse in the House
38 Panda in the Park
39 Tiger on the Track
40 Gorilla in the Glade
41 Tabby in the Tub
42 Chinchilla up the Chimney
43 Puppy in a Puddle
44 Leopard at the Lodge
45 Giraffe in a Jam
46 Hippo in a Hole
47 Foxes on the Farm
Hauntings 1: Dog in the Dungeon
Hauntings 2: Cat in the Crypt
Hauntings 3: Stallion in the Storm
Ponies at the Point
Seal on the Shore
Pigs at the Picnic
Sheepdog in the Snow
Kitten in the Cold
Fox in the Frost
Hamster in the Holly
Pony in the Post
Pup at the Palace
Animal Ark Favourites
Wildlife Ways

LUCY DANIELS

Dolphin
—— *in the* ——
Deep

Illustrations by Jenny Gregory

**Hodder
Children's
Books**

a division of Hodder Headline Limited

This edition of *Dolphin in the Deep* and *Whale in the Waves*
first published in 2000.

ISBN 0 340 78875 5
10 9 8 7 6 5 4 3 2

Dolphin in the Deep

Special thanks to Jenny Oldfield
Thanks also to C. J. Hall, B.Vet.Med., M.R.C.V.S., for reviewing
the veterinary information contained in this book.

Animal Ark is a trademark of Working Partners Limited
Text copyright © 1998 Working Partners Limited
Created by Working Partners Limited, London W6 0QT
Original series created by Ben M. Baglio
Illustrations copyright © 1998 Jenny Gregory

First published as a single volume in Great Britain in 1998
by Hodder Children's Books

For more information about Animal Ark, please contact
www.animalark.co.uk

A Catalogue record for this book is available from the British Library

Typeset by Avon Dataset Ltd, Bidford-on-Avon, Warks

Printed and bound in Great Britain by
Clays Ltd, St Ives plc

Hodder Children's Books
a division of Hodder Headline Limited
338 Euston Road
London NW1 3BH

One

'You know something? Right this minute I could be sitting watching a movie in a plane over the ocean!' Joel Logan sighed. He'd turned down a chance to fly with his grandmother to England.

Mandy Hope lay back, her arms behind her head, as their boat bobbed on a clear blue sea. 'Tough. Instead, you're stuck here in paradise.'

'Nothing to do, nowhere to go,' Joel moaned. He dipped his toe in the water. 'I must be crazy.'

'Why didn't you go, then?' Mandy rolled over on to her stomach. The deck of the boat was warm from the sun, the waves sparkled and danced. In the distance, she could see the tiny town of Dixie Springs perched at the edge of the bay.

''Cos . . .' He sat at the front of the launch, waiting for his grandfather, Jerry Logan, to start up the engine. They were drifting under the high sun, with not another boat in sight.

'Because you happen to like it here,' Mandy teased. 'Only it wouldn't be cool to admit you were having a good time.' That was how Joel was; pretending not to be interested in things like sponge fishing, which was what they were doing now.

'No way. It was 'cos I had to stay and look after Grandpa, keep him out of trouble,' Joel insisted. He perched on the edge of the boat, baseball cap pulled low over his tanned face.

'Yeah, sure.' His grandfather put down his pair of binoculars and took the wheel. 'And I had to stay home in Blue Bayous to take care of folks' gardens. Life's real hard.' He grinned as he choked the boat's engine back into life. 'Digging, weeding, planting, watering . . .' Though he was past seventy, Jerry Logan still ran Green Earth Gardens, his small gardening business. 'Guys my age should be taking things easy,' he joked.

'And I couldn't go back home with Gran and Grandad because you two needed someone to keep you both out of trouble!' Mandy joined in the joke. 'Tough decision.' She sighed and sat up, staring down into the deep blue water.

'Yeah, you could have been watching a movie with me, miles above the Atlantic.'

'Instead of messing about in Florida for an extra few weeks.'

'Back to British weather,' Jerry Logan reminded her.

'. . . Rain,' she agreed.

'Back to work,' Jerry added.

'. . . Helping out at Animal Ark for the rest of the summer holidays.' Cleaning cages, making appointments, visiting patients in the Yorkshire village of Welford with her parents, the local vets. Suddenly the joke went flat. Mandy had to admit that she did miss her mum and dad, and life at Animal Ark.

But she'd chosen to stay on when her grandparents flew home to Welford with Bee Logan. There was so much to do and see here in America, Mandy would have been mad to turn down the offer to stay longer.

'OK, time to head for home,' Jerry Logan decided. He choked the outboard motor back into life.

'But we didn't see any live sponges yet,' Joel complained.

Mandy had seen hundreds of them set out to dry on the harbourside at Dixie Springs. From a distance they looked like rows of brown coconuts or curled-up hedgehogs. Close to, you could see the delicate structure of the sponges.

' 'Cos you didn't dive to find them yet.' The easy-going old man didn't mind one way or the other. He steered the boat in a slow semi-circle to point towards the shore. 'Do you wanna do that now?'

Joel shrugged.

'Well, do you?' He turned to Mandy.

'Just to take a look. But how deep do we have to dive?'

'Until you get to the bottom,' he grinned.

'Are there lots?' She leaned over again to gaze down into the clear depths.

'Sure. Lucky for the divers, we don't allow tuna nets off Blue Bayous. That means all marine life gets protected. There's plenty of everything.' He explained how the big, commercial nets were illegal. 'Lucky for the dolphins too. If the waters get over-fished, there's nothing for them to eat.'

'Dolphins?' Mandy pricked up her ears. Dolphins sounded more interesting than sponges. Anything that breathed and moved, in or out of the water, was better than sponges as far as she was concerned.

'Yep, Dixie Springs is a good bay for them. They seem to like it.'

'How come?' Mandy knew the sea off the south-west coast of Florida was popular with bottlenose dolphins. But why especially Dixie Springs?

'They like the warm water,' Jerry explained.

'Me too. Let's go take a look.' Joel lifted his feet clear of the water and the boat set off.

'And in this bay they can do a spot of team fishing. See, they form a line and herd the fish towards the shore. Then they pick them off one by one.'

'Pretty clever.' Mandy was impressed. She scanned the waves for sleek grey shapes.

'Mostly at dawn and dusk,' Joel's grandpa continued. 'But I guess we could get lucky.'

It was midday. The sun glared overhead as the white boat cut through the blue sea.

'Over there!' Joel stood up and pointed.

'Where?' Mandy shot across to his side of the boat.

'Not there. There.' He pointed in a new direction.

'Where?' She concentrated so hard she almost fell over the side.

'Just kidding.' Joel grinned and swung under the silver rail into the tiny cabin. This was one of his favourite tricks.

'Do they really fish as a team?' Mandy had learned to ignore Joel's practical jokes.

'Yep, they're that smart.' Jerry Logan cruised across the bay. 'I've seen them doing it.' In his checked shirt, with his short grey hair and silver-rimmed glasses, he looked happy and relaxed.

In spite of the fact that Joel had tricked her, Mandy still kept her eyes peeled for dolphins. She was looking for their grey submarine shapes playing among the white spray made by their boat, or leaping out of the water ahead of them.

'What was that?' she said suddenly, craning over the edge. 'Joel, come and look.'

'Yeah, like I'm that stupid!' He sank into the seat in the shade of the canopy, refusing to budge.

'No, really. I think I saw something.'

'It's called the ocean.' Joel lay back, feet up, cap over his eyes.

'Yes, I did. There it is again!' She was sure this time. 'Slow down, Jerry. I can see two of them. Three, four!' They were shadows swimming up to the boat, deep underwater, twisting this way and that.

Hearing the note of excitement in her voice, Jerry Logan shut down the engine and let the boat drift.

Mandy leaned right out. '. . . Five, six! Honestly, Joel, you're mad to miss this!'

The sleek grey shapes were rising closer to the surface. They'd seen the boat and were coming to investigate. Now one was only a few metres away. Mandy could make out his fins, the strong up and down movement of his tail.

Joel snored, pretending to fall asleep.

'You should see him! He's over two metres long. And he's got this big round forehead and a long nose like a beak. I know this sounds silly, but it looks as if he's smiling at me!'

The dolphin poked his face up against the hull of the boat, then he turned on his back to show Mandy his pale belly. He scudded gently with his flippers, doing an easy backstroke.

'Yeah, yeah, yeah!' Joel opened one eye and peered out from under his cap.

'Here comes another one. It's much smaller. Maybe it's a baby!'

The young one was lively. He twisted under the boat, disappeared and then came tumbling back into view. His back fin broke the surface for a second, then vanished.

'Did you see that?' Mandy called.

'All I see is you making a fool of yourself.' Joel wasn't going to let Mandy get her own back. She could tell him there were *twenty* dolphins swimming around the boat and he still wouldn't move a muscle.

'OK, if you don't believe me, watch this!' She'd seen another playful dolphin join the first youngster and had an idea about what they planned to do next.

As Joel peered out from under his cap, the dolphins began to surge through the water towards

the boat. Mandy held her breath. Their fins thrust towards the surface, launching them out of the water in a burst of white spray.

Their bodies arched clear, then flipped sideways; one to the right, one to the left. A split second, and they were gone.

'Wow!' Joel jumped out of his seat. 'Did you see that? Two of them. They were *this* close!' He scrambled so fast to the side of the boat that he made it rock. 'What did I tell you? Didn't I say there were hundreds of dolphins in this bay?'

Jerry Logan glanced at Mandy and winked. 'Here come three more. They're real friendly. See that one giving the small guy a slap with her tail? She's keeping him in line. I guess she's the mother!'

Mandy grinned. It wasn't Joel changing his mind that was so funny. It was the sight of the dolphins. Everything about them; every flick of their tails, every glimpse of their curious smiling faces made her want to laugh and jump in the water to join them.

'It's a whole pod – a school of them.' Jerry too was enjoying the sight. 'Some of these youngsters are only a couple of months old, but they sure can move.'

'How fast?' She hung far out over the side, tipping the small boat.

'Around 30 miles per hour. I've seen them do more.' He'd lived all his life in Florida, except for the years he'd spent in England as a soldier. That was when he'd met Bee, married her and whisked her back to Blue Bayous. They'd raised a family here, and now every summer their grandson, Joel, came from New York to stay with them.

Mandy gasped as three more dolphins sped towards the boat. They dipped at the last minute and swam underneath, rising to the surface in a shower of sea spray. They poked their pointed noses at the boat and made gentle creaking noises.

'They're talking to you,' Jerry grinned. 'Try talking back.'

'How?' Mandy reached out to try to touch the nearest dolphin, but he flipped backwards out of reach.

'They like this kind of noise.' Jerry tapped the metal rail that Mandy was leaning against. 'It makes them curious.'

She tried it gently, tapping softly with her fingernails.

'Louder.'

Tap-tap-tap. She rattled her nails against the metal.

And all the dolphins came swimming up, swirling to the surface, making their own strange creaking noises, blowing hard through the blowholes on the tops of their heads. There were more than a dozen, rising and listening, chattering out an answer to the new sound.

'You can train these guys,' Joel told her, coming quietly alongside. 'They use a whistle to teach them tricks. I've seen it in the zoo.'

She shook her head. 'I don't think I'd like that.'

'How come?'

'Dunno. It sounds a bit cruel.' She never liked to see wild animals being tamed and taught to do cheap stunts.

'They like it. It's fun.' Joel shrugged and swung his legs and body under the rail.

'What are you doing?' Mandy was afraid Joel would scare the wonderful dolphins away.

'Going swimming. You coming?'

She glanced at Jerry, who nodded. 'No problem. I'll stick around until you're ready to leave,' he promised. He glanced up at the sun and chose a shady spot under the canopy.

By now Joel had lowered himself into the water and the dolphins were keeping their distance, checking out the new arrival.

'Can we?' Mandy asked, hardly able to believe their luck.

'Sure. They won't hurt you.' Jerry smilcd and nodded. 'There's never been a single recorded case of a dolphin making an unprovoked attack on a human being, and you're not about to be the first!'

'It's not that!' Mandy held her breath as she poised, ready to follow him.

Joel struck out, clear of the boat. 'They can kill a shark,' he yelled. 'They ram him in the side: *whack!*'

Mandy narrowed her eyes, looking for a clear space in the blue water. When she found one, she made a neat dive. Then she was in the sea, slicing through the water. Mandy dived under the surface, and felt the cool water welcome her. At last she opened her eyes – and found herself face to face with one of nature's most brilliant creatures.

The dolphin nosed against her, nudging her

gently. His beak was hard and his small eyes stared curiously.

Under the water Mandy stretched out her hand. The dolphin's head was smooth and firm, and when he rolled on to his back to let her stroke his belly, she felt the powerful muscles that propelled his body through the water. He curved his fins and rolled again, twisting upwards towards the sunlight.

Still holding her breath, she followed him. She kicked and broke the surface, drawing air into her lungs.

Nearby, Joel used a bold, noisy crawl to come up alongside two of the bigger dolphins who cruised side by side.

'Watch this!' he yelled. He made a lunge at the nearest dolphin. 'I'm hitching a ride!'

Mandy grinned as the dolphin slipped neatly out of reach. 'I don't think so!'

But Joel was persistent and the dolphins were good-tempered. They let him lunge again, waiting until he came up between them and managed to fling his arm round one of them. Then the dolphin set off across the bay, towing Joel in her wake.

'Yeah!' Joel yelled at the top of his voice. Spray

rose and shone in all the colours of the rainbow. It was better than the water rides in any theme park; faster, more daring, just fabulous!

Mandy looked on enviously.

But the dolphin who was towing Joel had a fine sense of humour. She took the boy far out to sea. She let him yell and shout and enjoy the trip. Then she dumped him. She came to a sudden stop and dived.

'Hey!' Joel had to let go. His yell turned to a wail. He was stranded a great distance from anywhere, paddling helplessly in the deep blue sea.

Jerry Logan grinned and started the motor. 'Jump aboard,' he told Mandy, leaning out to lend her a hand. 'We gotta sail to the rescue!'

And the school of dolphins came with them, making for the forward end of the boat, criss-crossing their bow wave, weaving from side to side.

Mandy sat on the deck, her fair hair dripping down her back, watching the dolphins play. *Trust Joel*, she thought. *Showing off, then getting dumped*.

He yelled for them to hurry. 'What took you so long?' he asked as his grandfather cut the engine and bobbed alongside.

The dolphins had formed a circle around the noisy, stranded boy. They seemed to grin as they opened their jaws and took in big mouthfuls of water.

'Uh-oh!' Jerry Logan warned. 'Watch out!'

Too late. The dolphins had Joel surrounded. They aimed and fired.

Half a dozen of the most playful ones were getting their own back as they squirted water at him. The jets rose like fountains and sprayed him from all directions. He disappeared beneath a torrent of sparkling drops.

'Gotcha!' Mandy grinned. Sometimes Joel deserved everything he got!

Two

'Have I ever rescued a dolphin?' Lauren Young repeated Mandy's question.

It was the day after the visit to Dixie Springs. Mandy and Joel had gone to help out at the rescue centre in the north of the island. GRROWL, or the Group for the Rescue and Rehabilitation of Wild Life, was run by Lauren, who was a qualified vet, together with a band of volunteers. They took in sick and wounded animals, nursed them back to health and tried to release them into their natural habitat.

'Yes. I mean, if there was a sick dolphin washed

up on the shore, would you be able to look after it?' Mandy knew that Lauren cared for racoons and squirrels, pelicans and turtles, deer and alligators. Everything that lived on Blue Bayous could find shelter here.

'That's a hard one.' Lauren examined an eagle's broken wing in one of the large cages in the yard of the rescue centre. The bird's head and tail were pure white, while its body and wings were dark. The eagle turned its head to peck at Lauren's hand with its hooked beak as she spread its mighty wing. But she held it expertly from behind, keeping out of harm's way.

'Why? Because they live in salt water?' The rescue centre was in the middle of a huge wilderness area with natural lakes and swamps, but Mandy didn't think a dolphin would be able to survive in the stagnant, brackish water.

'Yep. We'd need a special tank. If we heard about a dolphin getting sick, we'd probably call in a marine expert. We wouldn't treat it ourselves.' Lauren worked quickly to put the eagle back on its perch. Then she and Mandy stepped outside the cage.

The huge bird ruffled its feathers and poked its head in warning. It fixed them with its beady eyes.

Lauren, a young, slim woman with curly black hair, who reminded Mandy of her mum, turned to her. 'Why do you ask?'

'No reason.' Mandy went ahead, taking a bucket of fish to the cage of brown pelicans. Helping Lauren was one of the high points of her holiday here on Blue Bayous. Wall-to-wall sunshine, white beaches, blue seas and GRROWL. What could be better?

The ungainly pelicans waddled towards her, the slack pouches under their long beaks wobbling as they walked. They opened their mouths for food.

Mandy picked out a fish by its tail and flung it to the birds. Snap! The nearest pelican snaffled the prize.

Lauren stood outside the cage, arms folded. 'Joel tells me you went swimming with the dolphins yesterday.'

Mandy swung another fish and threw it. 'Did he tell you what they did to him?' She described the drenching Joel had brought on himself.

'I guess he forgot that part.' Lauren laughed.

'Never underestimate a dolphin, hey, Joel!'

Mandy emptied the bucket and turned to see him standing there, his face red. He'd brought Duchess, Lauren's Great Dane, down into the yard from the first-floor veranda.

'At least I hitched a ride before they got me.' It was more than Mandy had done.

'Call it their sense of fun.' Lauren patted the dog's head. 'I'd be kind of proud if it had happened to me. It means they like you.' She led them on to the racoon enclosure. 'You get other smart animals, like these little guys here, but for me a dolphin is unique.'

Mandy stared through the wire netting at a small group of racoons clinging to a stout tree branch. Their bandit faces peered back, their black hands grasped the branch and their striped tails swung to and fro. They were bright-eyed and alert.

'So what makes dolphins special?' Mandy asked. She realised how happy they made her feel when they surged towards her, but she wanted more hard facts.

'One; the dolphin is the only marine species to move its tail up and down instead of from side to side.' Lauren held up her forefinger and began to list the points. 'Two; they're known to have advanced forms of social behaviour.'

Joel made a dumb face. 'Huh?'

'They take care of one another. For instance, when a baby is born in April, a second female acts as midwife to the mother. She helps the calf to the surface so it can take its first breath, and she'll chase away any nearby sharks.'

'What else?' Mandy urged.

'Three; a dolphin's brain is larger than any other marine mammal's. In fact, it's the same size as a man's.'

'So they think like us? They're as smart as us?' Joel looked doubtful.

'Who knows?' Lauren shrugged. 'How do you measure intelligence? Some scientists will say a dolphin is only as smart as a dog or a chimp. Some say, no way; a dolphin is equal to a man any day.'

'Easily!' Mandy sighed. 'Only, how do you prove it?'

Lauren invited them upstairs for a sandwich and a cold drink. They were still talking dolphins half an hour later, sitting in the shade of the veranda on the cane chairs, waiting for Jerry Logan to call by and take them home.

'I heard a story once,' Lauren told them, 'about a young guy in a fishing boat way out in the Gulf of Mexico.'

Mandy eased back in her seat to listen, keeping one eye closed against the sun's glare, her feet resting idly on Duchess's broad back.

'The boat gets hit by a freak storm and turns over. The fisherman manages to cling to the hull, but there's no way he thinks anyone will come to rescue him. He knows the sharks will be around before too long. He spends a whole night out there, listening to things splashing in the black water all around. Sharks. It's only a matter of time . . .'

Mandy and Joel turned to Lauren, dreading the end.

'But the sun comes up and he sees it's not sharks making the splashes, it's dolphins. And they're doing it to keep the sharks away. He can see the man-eaters' fins slicing through the water, but they can't get at him because of the dolphins. Two days and two nights this goes on. He's dying out there from heat exhaustion. But the dolphins come right up to him and splash him to keep him awake. If he passes out, he'll slip into the water and the sharks will tear him to pieces.'

'What happened? Did they save him?' Joel asked.

'They sprayed him with water and waited until a boat arrived in the nick of time. He lived to tell the tale.'

'Do you believe that?' Joel wanted to know.

Lauren smiled and nodded. 'That man was my pa,' she confided.

Mandy sighed. She thought the story was mysterious and wonderful. 'It's kind of magic!'

'A miracle.' Lauren told them that if it hadn't been for the dolphins, she wouldn't be here now. 'My pa was twenty. He's nearly sixty now, but he still wears a chain round his neck with a gold charm in the shape of a dolphin. He swears he'll never take it off until he dies.'

In the silence that followed, Lauren shook herself and stood up, ready to go back to work. Duchess rose to her feet and plodded indoors.

'What are you thinking?' Joel asked Mandy. Even he had been impressed.

She squinted down at the yard. 'I'm thinking that

blue herons and brown pelicans and bald eagles are all very well,' she told him. 'I'm still mad about racoons and crazy about alligators . . .'

'But?'

'. . . It's dolphins from now on!' Dolphins in her dreams, gliding through turquoise water, diving to the coral reefs on the sea bed. Dolphins in the deep.

'How about meeting me at the rescue centre in half an hour?' A few days later, Lauren rang Mandy and issued an invite. 'Something came up. I have to drive to Ibis Gardens.'

'And you want us to come?' Mandy lolled at the kitchen table at Pelican's Roost, munching a cookie. Joel was next door at Moonshadow, swimming in the pool with Courtney Miller. It was a Saturday, five days after Gran and Grandad had flown back to England.

'Sure, if you'd like to. I'm taking Mitch back to Mel Hartley.'

'Who's Mitch?'

'A sea otter. Mel brought him to GRROWL a couple of days ago with a cut leg. He's fine now, though.'

'Hmm.' Sea otters were cute, but Mandy had promised Joel that she would join him and Courtney for a barbecue by the pool. Mrs Miller would be cooking right now. 'I don't know if I can.'

'OK, no problem.' Lauren was about to hang up. 'Some other time.'

'Ibis Gardens?' It was a theme park where there were all kinds of exotic animals: elephants, zebra and giraffe. Not so much a zoo as an 'African experience'. Mandy was tempted. 'Could we call in on Allie?'

Allie was an alligator who couldn't be trusted to be released into the wild since unwise tourists had fed him and turned him into a dangerous man-hunter. So they'd had to take him from GRROWL to live in a compound in Ibis Gardens. Mandy was keen to find out how he was getting on in his new home.

'Sure. Yes or no, Mandy? I have to hit the road.'

'Yes!' Mandy promised to get there double quick. She ran next door to find that the barbecue was off after all because Courtney had remembered a dentist's appointment.

So Joel jumped at the chance to come too, and

they took a lift from Mrs Miller. She said they had to drive past the rescue centre to keep her daughter's appointment.

'Sure you don't want to take my place at the dentist's?' Courtney grinned at Mandy as she climbed awkwardly out of the car. Her broken leg was still in plaster from an accident a few weeks before.

'Somehow I think he'd spot the difference!' Courtney had fair hair like Mandy, but the similarity ended there. She was tall and tanned and twice as glamorous.

'Have a good day!' Louise Miller called as she waved and drove off.

Mandy and Joel found Lauren in the yard, loading a small cage into the truck. She waved. 'Hi. Mitch would say hi too, but he's kind of upset. He doesn't like being locked up! I've had to take care of him here at GRROWL because the regular Ibis Gardens vet is on vacation.'

Mandy and Joel climbed in the back of the truck and peeped into the cage at the little sea otter. His blunt nose and whiskered face peered back. He had a thick brown coat and webbed feet; his broad tail thumped the floor of the cage.

'Hang on, we'll soon have you back home,' Mandy promised. They had a half-hour drive to the northern tip of the island. 'Does he have his own pool?' she called to Lauren, climbing into the driver's seat.

'No. He shares it.'

'Who with? More otters?'

'Nope. Mitch is the only one.' Lauren backed the truck out of the yard on to the rough track. Then she drove out on to the road.

'Who then?' Mitch was probably friendly and easy to get on with, except when he was sulking inside a cage.

'Bob and Bing.' Lauren relaxed. She rolled down the window and leaned an elbow against the door. They were on their way, past rows of sea-grape trees, across narrow wooden bridges that crossed flat, swampy streams. As always, the sun shone in a deep blue sky. 'This breeze is great,' she sighed.

'Who are Bob and Bing?' Mandy asked. The names were new to her. 'Are they sea lions?' Who could Mitch possibly share a pool with?

Lauren shook her head. 'No. Didn't I say?' Her

voice teased, as she glanced in her overhead mirror at the two curious faces in the back. 'Bob and Bing are a major attraction at Ibis Gardens. They're a couple of bottlenose dolphins!'

'Mandy, Joel, meet Bob and Bing.' The dolphin trainer, Mel Hartley, introduced his star duo. He stood at the side of the training pool with Mitch perched happily on his shoulder.

Mandy stared down into the green water, her heartbeat quickening as the two dolphins swam towards them. They came right under her nose, bobbing up with their heads tilted back, their beaks clapping together to make a hard rattling noise.

'They're saying hi!' Mel told them.

'Hi, Bob. Hi, Bing.' Joel knelt by the pool. 'Can we touch them?'

'Sure.' Mel wanted to talk to Lauren about Mitch, so he strolled away across the tiled poolside.

For a few seconds Mandy stood and watched. 'Which is which?' she wondered. To her, the two dolphins looked exactly alike, with their domed grey foreheads, small eyes set well back on the side of their heads, and their wide, smiling mouths.

'Who knows? Aren't they great?' Joel was stroking first one, then the other. 'Feel this, Mandy. It's not slimy like you'd think. But it's not dry either. It's kind of in-between.'

So she knelt beside him, feeling uneasy and excited at the same time. She reached out a hand to stroke the head of the nearest dolphin. He felt firm, smooth, and smelt of fish.

'It's not warm and it's not cold. It's kind of weird!' Joel rubbed his dolphin's nose.

Her dolphin paddled his flippers to stay in one place while they made friends. He creaked a message of rapid-fire sounds, bobbing within reach.

The noise made her grin. 'Hi,' she said softly. 'Is that what you're saying?'

'Can you believe this?' Joel tickled his dolphin under the chin. 'He's smiling at me!'

'Watch he doesn't spray you!'

'Who cares? I can't believe Lauren! She never even told us about these two!'

Mandy caught sight of the vet and the trainer across the other side of the small oval pool. Mel Hartley was about twenty-five years old, tall and well built. He looked like he spent a lot of time in the water with his animals. His wavy brown hair was short, his shoulders and chest were strong.

'Do you think they like it here?' Mandy asked Joel. 'You don't suppose the pool is too small?'

He shook his head. 'It's home.'

'I know. But that's what I mean. Compare it with living in the sea!' The pool sides were white and smooth, the water hygienically clean.

Joel saw what she was getting at. 'But they were probably born here. They don't know what they're missing, do they?' He'd seen plenty of dolphinariums, and none of the dolphins in them had ever looked unhappy, he told her.

'I'm not sure.' Mandy stood up and gazed down at the captive pair. 'If dolphins are as clever as Lauren says, don't you think they'd know they were being kept prisoner?' The thought bothered her more than she could say. And yet . . . Joel was right, they didn't seem sad.

Anyway, there was no more time to talk about it. Mel and Lauren had walked full circle round the training pool and come back to join them.

Mel put Mitch down at the poolside and they watched the little otter dive into the water. Soon he was sleek and happy, darting in-between his dolphin friends.

'Good news,' Lauren told Joel and Mandy. 'We arrived at exactly the right time.'

'How come?' Joel had shrugged off Mandy's worries. 'Is it feeding-time?'

'Better,' Lauren promised. 'Mel has to get Bob and Bing ready now. There's a dolphin show in the main arena five minutes from now. Come on, let's go see!'

Three

Bob and Bing sped like silent torpedoes through the tunnel from the training pool into the big arena. They surged to the surface and leapt three metres into the air in perfect unison.

'. . . Ah!' The crowd gave an enormous gasp.

As the dolphins plunged back into the water, the crowd leaned forward in their seats.

Up they came a second time, leaping and flipping backwards together, diving, twisting and jumping once more.

'Ooh! Aah!'

Water splashed over the rim of the pool. Perched

on their seats in the very front row, Mandy and Joel were soaked with spray.

Then Mel Hartley appeared through a doorway at the back of the arena. He waved at the crowd. The two dolphins surged out of the water, waving their flippers. Everyone clapped and roared.

'How do they do that?' Mandy gasped, eyes out on stalks. 'He didn't even give a signal!'

'Yes he did. See the whistle in his mouth?' Lauren pointed. 'It's high pitched so we can't hear it. But a dolphin can. They have a phenomenal sense of hearing.' She sat enjoying the crowd's amazement.

And now Mel gave another command, hard on the heels of the last one. He stood at the edge of the pool, waiting for Bing and Bob to surface. They appeared and rolled on to their backs, swam the length of the pool, twisted on to their bellies and scooted along the surface, smacking their broad tails on the water and splashing up white spray.

'Wow!' There was more applause, more cries of surprise as the dolphins went through their duet.

Mel dipped his hand into a box at the water's edge and drew out two small fish. He slipped them into Bob and Bing's open mouths at the end of the sequence. They swallowed them and swam quietly to the far side of the pool.

'Their reward,' Lauren smiled.

Mandy watched them take a rest, then glanced over her shoulder at the excited crowd. The arena sloped up behind her, row after row filled with tourists in colourful T-shirts and dark glasses, and hats to keep off the sun. It formed a huge semi-circle around the fifty-metre long pool, like a great sports stadium holding thousands of spectators.

'What do you think?' Joel nudged her with his elbow. 'Aren't they great?'

'Amazing!' Their timing was perfect, they obeyed every command.

And now it was time to show the crowd more tricks. Mel hoisted a bright yellow ball on the end of a wire across the water. Fixed to a pulley, it stayed six metres above the surface, swaying gently. He raised a hand to quieten the crowd. 'Bob wants to demonstrate how he plays a great game of basket-ball!' he announced. He pointed to a basket fixed to a board by the side of the pool. Then he signalled to one of the dolphins.

Mandy held her breath. Surely Bob couldn't get the ball into the basket?

The dolphin swam to a point directly under the yellow ball, then he gave a thrust of his flippers. He jumped, his streamlined body vertical; three, six metres clear. With a twist of his head, he knocked the ball with his nose. It sprang from its clip, curved through the air and fell neatly into the basket.

'Yes!' The crowd rose to its feet and roared.

'Did you see that!' Joel leapt up, speechless.

Mandy nodded. She pointed to the doorway behind Mel. A tiny dark brown figure had come trotting into view and up on to a wooden platform beside Mel. 'It's Mitch!' she whispered.

The little sea otter stood like an athlete on the winner's podium, head raised, soaking up the applause.

Bob swam up to him, rested against the side and spat a fountain of water all over the little pretender. It sent up a wave of laughter as the sea otter shook himself down and slunk off.

Then it was Bing's turn to do a special trick.

'Bing's game is water polo!' Mel announced. He

called the second dolphin across. 'He plays a pretty mean game too!'

This time it was a bright blue ball. The trainer took it from the box and spun it in his broad hand. Then he flipped it to the dolphin. Bing bobbed up to the surface and juggled it on the end of his nose, keeping it balanced as he swam along.

'No problem!' Mandy grinned.

'Pass it here, boy!' Mel ordered.

Bing shot the ball back with an accurate pass. Mel caught it, ran alongside and threw it back. Bing surged off.

'Now, pass!'

Bing did as he was told. He shot the ball sideways into the crowd. It soared over Joel and Mandy's heads. A girl four rows back jumped and caught it with both hands.

'Bad one!' Mel wagged his finger, pretending to be disappointed. Showing that his feelings were hurt, Bing went to sulk in a corner.

But the crowd was loving it. They urged the girl to throw the ball back into the pool for Bing to try again.

'Come on down!' Mel called. 'Bring the ball with you.'

Shyly the girl left her seat and came down the aisle. She was about eight years old with red hair tied back into a ponytail. She told Mel that her name was Kelly.

Mel squatted beside her. 'Kelly, do you think you can help me train Bing to make a better pass?'

The little girl nodded.

'OK. Now, blow into the whistle and get him to come.'

She blew. Bing was still sulking.

'Louder,' Mel urged.

This time the dolphin answered the call. He swam close to the spot where Kelly stood.

'OK, now throw him the ball.'

She tossed it. Bing caught it easily on the end of his nose.

'Tell him to pass it back.'

'Pass it here!' she murmured. When Bing went on juggling the ball, Kelly turned to look at Mel.

'Louder. Yell at him.'

She raised her voice. 'Pass it here!'

Suddenly Bing batted the ball neatly back. Kelly

caught it. But before the crowd could cheer, Bing himself beat them to it.

Jumping clear of the water, he did a victory roll, clapping his flippers together as he disappeared in a mass of bubbles. He swam underwater to join Bob at the far end of the pool.

The game had everyone calling out for more.

'They're a couple of comedians.' Lauren sat and grinned. 'What did I tell you; dolphins have a sense of humour!'

Mandy believed it. Seeing what she'd just seen, she would believe anything about dolphins. She shook her head. 'Look, here comes Mitch again!'

The sea otter was creeping back on to the winner's podium.

The audience spotted him and roared with laughter as Mel ordered him off.

'Aaah!' Mandy cried. She felt sorry for Mitch.

'Aaah, he's cute!' People nearby joined in.

Mitch paused.

'You want him to come back?' Mel called.

'Yes!' they cried.

So Mel let Mitch come back on to the podium to take the applause. He fed him with a scrap of fish

from the box. Meanwhile Bob and Bing swam quietly up and down the pool.

'Watch this!' Lauren leaned sideways to tell Mandy. 'Here comes the grand finale!'

She watched as Mel slid into the water between the dolphins. They greeted him with gentle nudges before all three dived below the foaming surface. For a few seconds all was quiet.

Then an amazing thing happened. The dolphins rose smoothly to the surface only centimetres apart. And there was Mel crouched astride them, straightening until he stood upright as the dolphins cruised the length of the pool. He spread his arms wide, balancing with one foot on Bob's back, one foot on Bing's. The crowd went wild.

'More!' they cried, as Bob and Bing parted and Mel sank between them. He swam to the side and climbed out, giving the dolphins their fish reward.

They dived, then leaped to do their victory roll. On the podium, the sea otter proudly took the applause.

'More!' The crowd chanted and stamped.

But the show was over. Mel waved and picked

Mitch up. They backed off towards the door, as the dolphins glided underwater, through the tunnel, out of sight.

'What a star!' Mandy watched Mitch swipe a fish from the pool in the special training compound behind the dolphin arena.

'Yep, he generally steals the show.' Mel Hartley was showing them round. For a moment the fish slipped and slid between the sharp claws of Mitch's webbed front paws. The otter snaffled it between his teeth and swallowed it.

'You want to take another look at the famous duo?'

'Bob and Bing?' Joel jumped at the chance. 'Can we feed them?'

'Sure. Follow me.' He led them back to the training pool with his easy, loping stride. 'How long have you got?' he asked Lauren.

'Till suppertime. I've got a volunteer standing in for me at the rescue centre.'

They went and crouched by the pool, looking for the dolphins.

'Over there.' Mandy spotted them resting close

to the surface, their triangular fins cruising through the water. 'How come they move their tails like that?' she asked Lauren. One thing about seeing them close to was that she got a chance to study their powerful bodies.

'It's because of the way the muscles are attached to the spine. Dolphins are mammals, remember. They're warm blooded. Ages ago they lived on the land, then they had to adapt to the sea. Their anatomy isn't the same as fish.' Lauren explained carefully, seeing that Mandy would gobble up any information she cared to give.

'And they breathe air?'

'Through the blowhole on the top of their heads. It's the same with all these guys, from the porpoise to the killer whale. They all belong to the same group.'

Joel frowned. 'Hey, I thought we were supposed to feed them,' he grumbled. 'Not get a science lesson!'

Mel grinned. 'That's what Bob and Bing think too. This is the special fish snack that I give them every day. The official ration is pretty strict, so I slip them a treat when no one's looking.' He winked and told them to watch.

The dolphins had swum up and circled impatiently, making the water lap over the edge of the pool.

Mandy felt it ooze through the sides of her trainers. 'How much do they eat?' she quizzed.

Mel laughed as he reached into the box for a fish and handed it to Joel. 'Another question!'

She blushed. 'Sorry, I can't help it.' She was always the same when she wanted to learn about a new animal.

Joel went more for the action. He held the fish by the tail and dangled it over the water, waiting for one of the dolphins to snatch. One rose and took it, then arched back into the water in one smooth movement. 'Who was that?'

'Bing. He has more white on his belly,' Mel replied.

'So, how much do they eat?' Mandy insisted.

'Too much, according to my boss! Bing is nearly three metres long and he weighs three hundred and fifty pounds. That's a lot of dolphin to maintain. So he eats about twenty pounds of fish in one day.' Mel knelt by the pool and slapped the water with the flat of his hand. The other dolphin came swimming up to him.

'Bob doesn't look quite so big,' Mandy said.

'More like three hundred pounds.' Mel leaned over to scratch the dolphin's head. 'He's not feeling so hot right now. Are you, boy? I have to persuade him to eat.' He reached for a fish and slipped it into his mouth. 'See how he swallows it head first?'

Mandy caught a glimpse inside Bob's wide mouth and saw a set of ridged, interlocking teeth like a zip fastener. But Bob didn't chew his food. He turned the fish so it went down head first, as Mel had said.

'And they don't mind living in a dolphinarium?' Mandy let the question slip. It was on her mind all the time she watched the show; the idea that the beautiful dolphins were somehow treated like freaks.

Mel narrowed his eyes and glanced at her. 'How should I know? I never asked them,' he said shortly. He stood up and went to fetch a fresh bucket of fish from the cool store.

Lauren raised her eyebrows at Mandy. 'Nice one, Mandy. Bob and Bing have worked with Mel for five years, since they were babies. They were born at Ibis Gardens, and lived with their mom until she died last fall.'

'Sorry.' She blushed, then sighed. 'But it's just like Mel said: we can't ask them if they like it, can we?'

They stood gazing at the pair of tame dolphins swimming up and down, up and down the length of the twenty-metre pool.

'Tell you what!' Mel said, in a better mood when he came back with the fresh load of fish. 'Since Mandy here isn't so sure that my dolphins have a nice life, why not stick around and see for yourselves?'

'How do you mean, stick around?' Joel tilted his head to one side. He was hungry, and just about ready to go back to Pelican's Roost with Lauren.

'Stay over. That is, if you're not doing anything for the next couple of days.'

'And help here?' It was Mandy's turn to jump in quickly. 'Can we?' She turned to Lauren.

'I guess. They could stay in the staff quarters if Mr Boston agrees, couldn't they?'

Mel nodded. 'No problem. I just have to tell him we've got a couple of willing helpers working for nothing. He'll say yes right away.'

'Will Boston is Mel's boss,' Lauren explained. 'He owns Ibis Gardens. Most of the staff live in.'

'Where?' Mandy had only seen the tourist bit of the theme park: the enclosures for the gorillas, the compounds for the tigers and the islands in the middle of the lake where the monkeys lived.

'At the back of the park. It looks like a motel, and it's pretty basic.' Mel told them what to expect. 'No luxuries.'

'Do we get a TV?' Joel wanted to know.

Mel grinned. 'Sure. But if you stay, I'll work you so hard you won't have time to watch it!'

'How about it?' Lauren was looking at her watch. 'Do you want to phone your grandpa and ask if it's OK?'

Still Joel hesitated. 'We work for nothing?'

'I'll give you your food and board. And a whole new look at the life of a dolphin!'

'Can we help with the shows?' Joel asked. 'Will Bob and Bing perform their tricks for us?'

Mandy grew impatient. She would have said yes ages ago. Two or three days living with dolphins; feeding them, cleaning their pools, maybe even swimming with them, and definitely learning everything there was to know. Why on earth was Joel being so cagey?

'They will if they trust you,' Mel told him, looking them both in the eye. 'But if they don't like you, no way!'

This was a challenge even Joel couldn't back out of, Mandy knew.

'OK,' he agreed at last. 'Let's phone home and tell Grandpa we want to stay!'

Four

'What is it with you and the dolphins?' Mandy asked Mel. She dangled her legs over the side of the training pool, watching him teach them a new trick.

The idea was for Bob and Bing to swim side by side, with Mel in the middle. He was to give three blows on the whistle, then grab each dolphin by the nearest flipper. Then they would tow him through the water at high speed. After only two tries, they'd got the hang of it. Now they did it perfectly each time.

'I guess I don't really know.' Mel hauled himself out of the pool and sat beside her. Water streamed from his wetsuit as he leaned over to throw the dolphins two small fish. 'But it's something special. Some kind of bond that you can feel but can't put into words. I just know how lucky I am to have them trust me the way they do.'

Mandy nodded. She liked Mel, she decided. She wished she could say the same about Will Boston, the owner of Ibis Gardens, who strode towards them now. It was first thing on Sunday morning, before the park had opened.

'Hey, how's it going?' he said briskly. He carried a rolled-up newspaper which he tapped against his leg all the time he spoke.

'Hey, Will,' Mel said without looking up. He was studying Bob as the dolphin turned away from the fish he was offered.

'I was just talking to the kid, Joel.'

Mandy squinted up at the boss of Ibis Gardens. The sun had risen behind his shoulder, leaving his face in dark shadow. But she could tell from his voice that he wasn't pleased. She imagined a frown, a mouth turning down at the corners behind that bushy black moustache, and she could also tell that he and the dolphin trainer didn't get on.

'The kid says you're not happy with Bob. What's wrong? Is he sick or something?'

'I don't know yet.' The trainer stood up, hands on hips. 'He's not eating much.'

Will Boston grunted. 'He looks fine to me.'

'Yeah.' Mel stooped to sprinkle water over Bob's back as the dolphin rose to the surface for air. 'Maybe it was something he ate. Some kind of stomach bug.'

'Or maybe he's fooling you, wanting you to feel sorry for him so he doesn't have to work.' The boss made it clear he wouldn't stand any nonsense. 'These dolphins are smart, remember. But I can't afford to have one of them falling sick.'

'Yeah, yeah.' Mel had heard it all before. 'We know that, don't we, Bob? Four shows a day, six days a week. Tell Mr Boston there's no reason to worry.'

Bob creaked an answer from deep in his throat. Mandy hid a smile. It sounded for all the world as if the dolphin had understood exactly what Mel had said.

'The show's nothing with only one of them out there. We need two. That's the way we advertise it, as a double act, and right now we can't afford to rest them.'

Mandy heard Will Boston scratch the stubble on his chin as he rubbed his hand up and down his face. She'd taken a dislike to him the moment she saw him. It wasn't his stocky, short-legged figure, nor his bristling moustache. She knew other men like that without wanting to run a mile. It wasn't even his high-pitched, whiny voice. It was the dead look in his eyes as he bossed people about, that way he had of not looking directly at anyone.

Now he noticed her sitting there. 'You hear that? Don't let these guys fool you. Let them know who's boss.'

Mandy couldn't think of any reply, so she smiled foolishly instead.

'The other kid, Joel; he says you're from England?' She nodded.

'Well, I hope you're gonna go back home and tell folks what a great place we have here at Ibis Gardens. Major attractions. "Little Africa", we call it. Why go through the hassle of the real thing when you can jump on a plane and fly right here?' He whacked the newspaper against his leg and aimed it at her like a gun. 'What do you say?'

Afraid to say anything, Mandy nodded again.

'OK, well that's great.' He glanced at his watch. 'First show of the day in half an hour. You make sure this dolphin's in good shape for me, you hear?' He altered his sights to rest on poor Bob.

'Sure thing,' Mel said in sharp response.

Mandy felt she should stand to attention as the owner of Ibis Gardens rapped out his opinions.

Will Boston was satisfied that he'd got his message across. He lowered his newspaper to his side. 'You have a nice day now,' he said as he pulled Mel to one side.

Mandy was glad to be left in peace with the dolphins. She'd spent a restless night in her room, listening to the noisy air conditioning. The bare, stuffy room had made her feel a long way from home.

But as soon as she'd got up and had breakfast of blueberry muffins and hot chocolate, she'd come out with Mel and Joel to say hi to Bob and Bing. Already she felt better. Just to see them rise to the surface to greet her, watching the water roll off their broad backs, seeing them breathe, made her feel glad to be alive.

What is it with me *and dolphins?* She changed the question she'd put to Mel a little earlier.

'Is it the way you swim?' she asked out loud. 'Or the way you always want to play?'

'You know what they say?' Joel came up suddenly from behind.

Mandy jumped. 'No, what?'

'About talking to yourself. It means you're going crazy.' He sat and dangled his bare legs in the water.

'I wasn't talking to myself, I was talking to Bob and Bing.'

'Same thing,' he shrugged.

'No, it's not,' Mandy said. 'Didn't you know that talking to dolphins can be a whole lot more enjoyable than talking to some people?' She could prove it right there and then. 'You want to see?'

Without waiting for an answer, she took the whistle that Mel had left on the fish box and hung it round her neck. Then she jumped into the pool.

The dolphins reacted with a warm welcome, swimming up quickly and nudging her. Mandy tried not to be nervous, remembering how Mel behaved with them. For a few minutes she just swam, letting them get used to her being there.

'So?' Joel demanded. 'What am I looking at?'

'Wait.' She decided it was time to put the whistle to her lips and give three short blasts. Would it work?

Yes; Bing came alongside, and then Bob. She was in the middle. The dolphins were offering her their flippers so that she could hold on. Then they were kicking with their tails, surging along the surface, gathering speed. They towed her between them. Mandy felt the water part in a great wave, felt the splash of spray, then the gentle let down as the two dolphins came to a halt. They swam apart to let her sink deep into the clear blue water.

When she came up again, Mel was standing beside an astonished Joel.

'Pretty good!' Mel clapped slowly. 'Let's keep it in the act!'

Out of breath, amazed that the trick had worked, she clambered out of the pool. 'What do you mean?'

'Keep it in,' he repeated. 'You did real good.'

'Me?' Mandy stared back at him. 'Do that in front of a whole crowd?' Her knees went weak at the idea.

'Sure. Why not?' Mel grinned and slapped her on the back. 'You got the dolphins on your side; now you can get them to do any trick you like!'

'OK, Mandy, way to go!' Joel urged.

There was a sea of faces in the arena. Mel had introduced her as his guest assistant. She stood dressed in a grey and blue wetsuit for this last show of the day.

'You OK?' he whispered.

Her legs trembled, her mouth felt dry. 'I wish I'd never agreed to this!'

Mitch the sea otter was doing his thing of sneaking up on to the podium. The crowd roared with laughter.

'Go for it!' Joel gave Mandy a small shove so that she stood in full view of everyone. The audience spotted her and began to clap and shout.

'This girl is fabulous with animals, believe me!' Mel told them.

Mandy stared at the rows of people. It was all a blur of bright colour and noise, rising to the back of the arena. She spotted Will Boston leaning on the rail at the front, waiting nervously for her to perform, obviously pinning his hopes on her to thrill the crowd. There was no backing out now.

So she ran and dived neatly into the pool, came up and whistled for the dolphins. They came at her call, turning to have their tummies tickled and nudging against her to say hi. She stroked them, and Bing offered her his flipper. Together they paddled to the middle of the pool.

Soon Mandy found that she could ignore where she was. All she knew was that she was with the dolphins, proud to be their friend. She relaxed. The trick would go fine. Bob and Bing wouldn't let her down.

'Ready?' she asked as Bob followed them across the pool. She put the whistle to her mouth and gave the short signal, waiting for the dolphins to settle into position. Then she seized their flippers and waited for them to set off.

Their strong tails began to churn through the water, the waves parted ahead of them and they were off. Mandy held tight. They raced the length of the pool, spray flying, the cool water washing against her.

There was a cheer, and cries for Mandy to do it

again. So she waited for the dolphins to turn, then gave a second signal. They towed her back down the pool in triumph.

When it was over, Mel and Joel reached out their hands and hauled her out. 'Terrific!' Mel congratulated her.

Mandy turned and took a bow, grinning as Mitch stole the limelight from the top of his platform. She heaved a deep sigh.

'I knew you could do it!' Joel was pleased for her.

Mandy even saw Will Boston give her a thumbs-up sign, relief written all over his dark features.

'Thanks to Bob and Bing!' Mandy gasped, glad that it was over, proud that they'd done it. She remembered to dip into the box for their fish reward and patted their heads as Bing came up to feed.

'Come on, Bob!' Joel coaxed.

But the smaller dolphin was still off his food. The show continued, rolling on with the next trick, thrilling the audience. When it was over and the dolphins had made their final leap before they swam off down the tunnel, Will Boston came hurrying across.

'Great! Keep it in!' He beamed at Mandy. 'The crowd loved you! Word will get round and takings will go up! Who knows, you could help Ibis Gardens get over our small financial problem.'

Mandy blushed, promising to do it again next day.

'If Bob is up to it,' Mel reminded them. He'd unzipped his wetsuit and slung a towel around his neck. 'I'm getting concerned. He's definitely not eating enough, and he's slowing down.'

Will Boston shrugged it off. 'Quit worrying. He looks fine to me. If he was sick, he wouldn't want to do the shows.'

'Maybe. But Bob likes to please. I reckon he'd keep going even if he felt lousy.' The trainer shook his head and sighed.

'Forget it!' His boss blustered his way through. 'I want this kid to keep the trick in, OK?'

'Listen, Will, how about giving Bob a couple of days off?' Mel refused to be beaten down. 'I think he needs it.'

'No way!' came the rapid reply. 'What, and let thousands of people down?' He spread his hands, palms upwards. 'What can I do? They come to see dolphins, and dolphins is what they're gonna see!'

He turned on his heel and marched off, muttering to himself. 'Who does this guy think he is? Telling me the fish needs a break!'

'Bob isn't a fish!' Mandy protested.

'He knows it.' Mel was still shaking his head. 'All he thinks about is dollar signs; money, money, money! Come on, let's get out of here. How about I take you guys for an ice cream up at the Springs? We could all use a break, and there's just time to drive up to Dixie before sunset.'

'Great idea, thanks!' To Mandy, the idea of sitting

by the bay at dusk, eating ice cream, not to mention watching for wild dolphins, was too good to be missed!

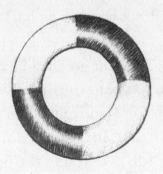

Five

The red sun was low in the sky. It cast a pink glow over the white houses of Dixie Springs, as Mandy, Joel and Mel picked their way between the rows of sponges set out along the quay.

'Can we take a boat out?' Joel asked. They'd finished their chocolate chip ice creams and were taking a stroll along the pier, looking for dolphins. There was just time to do a circuit of the bay before the sun sank out of sight.

'Sure.' Mel seemed to have his mind on other things. 'You and Mandy go. I'll wait here.'

'Is that OK?' Mandy checked. Mel still looked

worried. 'You don't want to go back and find out how Bob is?'

Mel smiled. 'No, you go ahead.' He spoke to a fisherman who was pottering in his boat, and fixed up a quick trip for Mandy and Joel. 'See you!' he called. 'Watch out for those dolphins. Steve Peratinos here will take you to the best places. He keeps a log. Ask him.'

Soon they set off, and curved across the still water towards the setting sun. Their fisherman was a friendly old man with strong, wiry arms and broad hands that gripped the wheel. He wore a faded denim cap, and his face was lined from years in the sun.

'What kind of log do you keep?' Mandy asked. Every ripple in the sea's smooth surface promised a dolphin sighting, but so far they hadn't been lucky.

'I write down how many dolphins I see, what they do, which direction they swim in. Stuff like that.' Steve Peratinos swung the boat round towards the far shore. 'We set up a Dolphin Watch last year.'

'Who's we?' Joel asked. The breeze blew through his T-shirt and against the peak of his cap, so he decided to turn it around and wear it back to front.

'Guys who fish round here. And the coastguards, a couple of scientists from Orlando . . . you know.' Steve's deep, gravelly voice drifted on. 'The best time is around spring, when they have their young. That's when the count shoots way up!'

'I guess we missed it.' Joel moved restlessly around the edge of the boat, peering down.

'Over there!' Mandy pointed to an area close to the shore. She'd spotted dolphins.

Steve altered course. 'Yeah, you missed that part,' he explained, 'but the young calves are still around. You might hit lucky.'

'We already did.' Mandy pointed again. Two dolphins had risen to the surface close by; a mother and her offspring by the look of things. 'Isn't that great?'

She saw how the calf shadowed its mother, rising for air then diving out of sight. Then there were more dolphins, weaving through the bow wave of their boat, playing in the spray. 'How old is the calf?' she asked.

'Four months, maybe five.'

'It's quite big already.' The calf was almost as long as its mother, but much thinner.

'How long do they stay together?'

'Mother and calf? Let's see. The young guy won't leave her side until he's six months old. Then he'll go off to catch a few fish. But he won't be weaned until he's a year and a half old.'

'Wow! Did you see that?' Joel shot across the boat to the far side. 'Three of them jumping way out. Did you see it?'

'Sit down, you're rocking the boat!' Steve warned him, then he went on explaining to Mandy about the young calf. 'He feeds on milk, just like you and me.'

Mandy frowned. 'Underwater?'

Steve laughed. 'It's kind of neat. Mom has a slit in her belly. When she wants to feed the baby, out pops the nipple.'

'P-lease!' Joel cried, pretending to cover his ears.

Steve went on: 'And the calf's tongue kind of makes a tube when he presses it against the roof of his mouth. He puts his mouth to the nipple, Mom squirts milk into the tube, and there you go. One pretty neat system, hey?'

'Amazing!' Mandy marvelled. Another mystery solved.

'Hey!' Steve cried, as Joel ignored their conversation and flung himself back across the boat for a better view of the acrobatic dolphins. 'Steady!'

But the warning came too late. The boat rocked from Joel's reckless leap. He overbalanced and tried to catch hold of the rail.

'Grab him!' Steve yelled at Mandy. 'He's going over!'

She lunged and touched Joel's fingertips as the boat tilted and he slipped away, across the wet deck. The next second, he was gone.

Stung into action, Steve cut the engine. 'Man overboard! Can you see him?'

Over the side, down in the deep blue water, there was a froth of bubbles rising to the surface, but no sign of Joel himself. 'No! He's gone under!' cried Mandy.

The three playful dolphins gave up their game and vanished. Four or five others swam quietly nearby.

It was as if time stood still. Mandy stared down at the rising bubbles, stunned by what had happened.

Then Steve unhitched the lifebelt and threw it

into the water. 'Did he hit his head?' he yelled at Mandy.

'I don't know. It happened too quick.' She was kicking off her shoes, ready to jump into the sea. Someone had to dive down there and see.

'Hold it!' Steve was there beside her, holding on to her arm. The boat still bobbed dangerously. He didn't want a second emergency if Mandy were to leap out into danger.

She strained to get free. 'Please!' she begged. 'He could drown!'

'Wait!'

There in the blue water, from way down deep, shapes were rising.

'See!' Steve hung over the side and pointed through the surge of bubbles.

Yes; something was coming to the top, rising closer and closer. Mandy could make out wide tails, long snouts; the young dolphins bunched together lifting a pale shape between them. Joel! His body looked limp as it broke the surface.

The water drained off him as the three dolphins buoyed him up. The sudden light hit him and he moved. Mandy saw him take in a great gasp of air.

Thank heavens! Now Steve let go of her and she jumped over the side. She hooked her arm through the lifebelt and swam with it. 'Grab this!' she told a dazed Joel, swimming between the three dolphin rescuers.

He was shocked, but able to do as he was told. He struggled into the belt and flopped back, breathing deeply.

Mandy held on to him, and towed him towards the boat. Sure that he was safe, the dolphins backed away. She thanked them silently, but out loud, she told Joel off.

'What do you think you were doing?' she cried, clinging to him with one hand, and hanging on to the side of the boat with the other. She waited for Steve to haul him back on board. 'You were down there ages. We thought you'd drowned!'

'I must have blacked out.' Joel slumped across the deck, his legs dangling. 'I don't remember.'

'Lucky for you, the dolphins knew you were in trouble,' Steve told him. He helped pull Mandy to safety.

With both of them back, breathing heavily, shocked but all in one piece, they gazed out to sea.

The sun was a fiery ball on the orange horizon. Streaks of pale gold clouds streamed across the sky. The water shimmered silver. And there, criss-crossing the bay, leaping and diving, were the wonderful dolphins who had rescued Joel: a trio swimming in harmony, disappearing into the distance.

Steve nodded and turned the engine on. He told Mandy to keep an eye on Joel to make sure he didn't do any other fool thing, then he swung the boat to face the shore.

He shook his head as he thought of the narrow escape. 'That sure is one for the log!' he said.

'The amazing thing was, these dolphins were completely wild,' Mandy told Lauren Young on the telephone. 'They knew nothing about us humans. Yet they realised straight away that Joel was in trouble. How?'

She was sitting with Joel in the cramped staff quarters at Ibis Gardens. Mel had insisted that they rang Jerry Logan to tell him what had happened, even though Joel said he was perfectly fine now. He'd even made him stay inside to rest.

'It's only eight o'clock,' he'd complained.

It was already dark, with a muggy feel to the air. There was no breeze and there was a thick covering of mist which had rolled in from the sea.

Anyway, here he was grounded, following his grandpa's anxious orders, and there was Lauren from the rescue centre on the other end of the line.

'How did they know he needed rescuing?' Mandy asked again.

'It's uncanny, isn't it?' Lauren agreed. 'Like they have a sixth sense. They really are the most wonderful creatures!' She checked once more that Joel had survived the experience unscathed. Then she asked Mandy to put Mel Hartley back on the phone.

'What is this?' Joel asked. 'Why the big deal?'

'No big deal. Those three dolphins only saved your life, that's all!' Mandy pushed her hair back from her face and tried to listen in to Mel's conversation with Lauren.

'. . . Yeah, I guess you'd better come over first thing tomorrow,' Mel told her. '. . . I don't like it. . . . No, our resident vet is still on vacation and I can't get hold of anyone else right now. Could you come?'

Say yes! Mandy prayed. She too was worried.

'You know what the boss here is like,' Mel went on. 'It's crazy. He won't spend money on good fish for the dolphins; he buys the cheap stuff. Sometimes I think it's no wonder Bob's gone off his food. And Boston keeps on telling me the Gardens is in financial trouble, that's why he can't afford to give the dolphins a rest.'

Mandy frowned. 'How come? That doesn't make sense; the crowd for the show is always huge,' she whispered to Joel.

He shrugged. 'Don't ask me. Say, did the wild dolphins really save my life?'

'Yep.' How many times did he need to be told?

There was a pause. 'Wow!' Another pause.

Mandy strained to hear Mel.

'Boston's so tight with money I buy extra fish for Bob and Bing out of my own salary. I've been telling him he'll have to spend more ever since last fall, when we lost Dorothy, Bob and Bing's mom. Same problem; I know she got sick because of the cheap food we were giving them. Of course, the guy won't listen . . .'

'This is more serious than we thought!' Mandy listened with a knot of worry growing in her stomach. The dolphins obviously needed to be fit and happy to be able to work well in the show. 'What if the same thing starts to happen to Bing as well?'

Joel shook his head. 'Maybe we can persuade Mr Boston to get some help.'

Mandy doubted it. Expert help cost money. 'We're going to have to go behind his back,' she warned.

Obviously Mel agreed. '. . . So you'll come over?' he said to Lauren at last. 'OK, we'll see you first thing in the morning!'

'What do you mean, you can't do anything for him?' Will Boston was yelling at Lauren Young.

It was early on Monday morning. Lauren had driven over from the rescue centre as dawn broke. Now she stood by the dolphins' training pool in the middle of a huge row with Will Boston.

Mandy heard him shout and broke into a run. She'd woken up early, listening for Lauren's truck to drive past the staff quarters. The moment she'd heard it, she'd quickly slipped into her shorts and T-shirt and headed straight for the pool. But it seemed she'd already missed the vet's verdict on Bob.

Lauren stood her ground, folding her arms and letting the owner of the theme park finish before she answered. 'He's got a high fever,' she explained. 'He's slow and listless. And he's not been eating properly for the last few days. He's sick for sure.' She glanced apologetically at Mel, who stood next to her, arms folded, with a worried expression.

'So, what's he got?' Boston demanded.

'I can't say. I'm no dolphin expert. You need a second opinion.'

'And my vet's on vacation. I don't have the money to spend on bringing in a marine expert. Just give us a clue; what do you think it is?'

'Could be a virus. Or it could be something to do with the type of food he's getting.' She shrugged and turned back to Mel. 'How old is he?'

'Five and a half, nearly six. That's no age for a dolphin. They can live up to forty years.'

'This is crazy!' Will Boston raised his voice still further. 'I'm paying you to tell me the dolphin's got the flu?' His face was red with frustration as he thought of the problems it would cause with the daily shows.

'I didn't say that,' Lauren said calmly. 'It could be his diet, remember. I'm saying you need to bring in an expert. I know a guy from upstate, but it could take him a couple of days to get here. A lot of people call him for help. I know; I phoned him to check.'

'A couple of days?' The boss's jaw fell open. 'What are we supposed to do? Close down until your so-called expert can get here?'

She nodded. 'That's my advice.'

'No way!' he warned Mel. 'You didn't hear her say that, OK? It's a complete disaster if we have to close the show. No one pays money to come

through those gates unless they know for sure they're gonna see Bob and Bing!'

Mel hung his head and muttered.

'Look, I'm doing my best here, OK!' Lauren turned away with a shake of her head. 'I'm telling you you've got a sick animal. Pretty darned sick, as a matter of fact.'

Mandy bit her lip. This was the first time anyone had admitted they were really worried about Bob, and she knew from what she'd seen at Animal Ark how quickly animals could go downhill once they fell ill. She felt her chest go tight with fear.

Even Mr Boston was stopped short. 'What are you saying? This illness; is it bad?'

Lauren spread her hands. 'I don't know. Get Matt Greenaway to come down from Orlando. He'll give you a proper diagnosis. Meanwhile, I'd say you should keep the dolphin in isolation, in case he's infectious.'

'You mean the other one could catch it too?'

'Maybe. It's best to play it safe from now on.'

'Cancel the shows?' There was a wobble in Will Boston's voice.

'For sure.' She gave her advice, rolled down her

sleeves, told Mel she was sorry that there was nothing else she could do.

The trainer turned to reason with his boss. 'The fact is, Mr Boston; if Bob here gets any worse – if he isn't given time off and a chance to recover – there isn't going to *be* any Bob and Bing show ever again!'

'Don't give me that!' The plea fell on deaf ears. 'I know you dolphin people; you think the least little snuffle means the end for them. You want to pamper and spoil them, as if nothing else matters. Well, I've got a whole park to run, and it's not easy.' He turned to Lauren. 'So no more talk of isolation and cancelling the show,' he insisted. 'Let's just see how it goes!'

Mandy had heard enough. She didn't wait to say goodbye to Lauren, but went off instead to visit Bob and Bing.

The dolphins were swimming quietly at the far end of the pool. They didn't rise through the water to greet her, so she knelt and slapped the surface. Bing came up slowly, sucked in air and let himself be patted. But there was no liveliness in him this morning, no mischief. Soon he turned and dived back to the bottom to join Bob.

She sighed. 'What's wrong?' she murmured into the wavy depths.

There was silence, except for the lapping of the water against the side of the pool. Of course, a dolphin couldn't talk back. Not in any language she understood.

Then she heard the patter of webbed feet across the tiles, and here was Mitch, out of his cage, scurrying towards her. Mel followed more slowly.

'What do you want?' Mandy said to the sea otter with a smile. Tame as could be, he scrambled on to her lap.

'He wants to play,' Mel said, gazing down at the shadowy shapes of his two dolphins. 'I wish we could say the same about Bob.'

The sick dolphin rose feebly to the surface for air. He blew faintly and looked at them with weary, half-closed eyes. Then he turned heavily and dived to the bottom again.

'So do I,' Mandy sighed. She'd never wished so hard for anything in her life.

Six

They separated Bob and Bing as soon as Lauren had left. She'd advised a shot of antibiotics for Bob, just in case it helped. And when she'd given him the injection, she insisted that he needed to be in a pool by himself.

'Won't they get lonely?' Mandy had asked. The two dolphins spent all their time together. If they were separated, both Bob and Bing would be sure to pine.

Lauren had admitted Mandy could be right. 'But what can we do? The last thing we want is for Bing to get sick too.' Keeping Bob in isolation was the only way.

So Mel decided to keep the sick dolphin in the smaller training area, while Bing was put into the main show pool.

'See, he doesn't want to go!' Mandy watched the trainer trying to herd Bing towards the tunnel. The dolphin would swim slowly up to it, then stubbornly turn tail and go back to Bob.

'I'm sorry.' Mel was just as determined. 'If the vet says we have to take you away from him, it's for your own good, you hear!' He tried again. Again Bing swam to the narrow entrance, then heaved up out of the water, flipped on to his back and rolled down to join Bob once more.

Mandy watched sadly. Tears came into her eyes as she watched Bing sticking faithfully by Bob's side. Poor Bob was hardly moving from the far corner of the pool, but he did seem to greet Bing with a nudge and a flip of his tail whenever the bigger dolphin returned to his side.

'You don't suppose they know best?' she murmured. 'Lauren could be wrong about Bob being infectious.'

'I can't risk it,' Mel decided. He didn't like this any more than Mandy did. 'You'd better jump into the pool with me. The two of us might be able to get him through the tunnel.'

Reluctantly Mandy dived in and swam underwater. She kicked hard, keeping her eyes open, until she reached the dolphins. Bubbles of air escaped from her nose as she twisted and came alongside Bob. She put her arm around him and stroked his nose. Feebly he flicked his tail and leaned his head against her. Bing paddled gently nearby, watching Bob's every movement, refusing to leave him.

Mandy needed air, so she kicked upwards and broke the surface.

'Bing really doesn't want to go,' she pleaded. 'He realises there's something wrong!'

'I know.' Mel got ready to dive under. 'But we can't ignore Lauren. What we'll do is both dive down and swim to either side of Bing, OK? We'll grab a flipper each to show him we mean business. He's strong enough to shake us off if he wants to, but he trusts us enough to do it our way. We keep hold of him and guide him to the tunnel. Once he's got his nose in there, we'll block his way back. That way he'll have to swim forward and we close the door after him.' He waited to see that Mandy had understood. 'Got that?'

She nodded and took a deep breath.

'Come on, let's do it!'

Mel disappeared below the glittering surface and Mandy followed. They kept to the plan, and when they had hold of Bing's flippers, they began to ease him away from Bob. For a few seconds Mandy expected him to resist. But though he turned his head to look back at Bob he decided to let the humans have their way. They eased him towards the tunnel, gently pushed him through head first, and at last slid the door shut behind him.

With her lungs aching, Mandy shot towards the light. Her head and shoulders burst out of the water and she gasped for air. Mel was by her side, telling her she'd done well. 'I couldn't have done that without you!'

Mandy shook her head. 'How come I feel so bad then?' She remembered that last look that Bing had given Bob. It was as if he knew he was saying goodbye for good.

'Let's take a break.' Mel swam for the side. 'I have to report to the boss.'

They climbed out together. 'I'll stay,' Mandy decided. 'Are you going to tell him we'll definitely have to cancel?'

'Yep. He'll go ballistic, but what can we do?' Mel trudged away to deliver the bad news to Will Boston. 'I'm gonna get on the phone to Matt Greenaway one more time,' he called back. 'I haven't been able to get through yet, but we need him down here just as soon as he can make it!'

He disappeared and left Mandy alone by the pool. By now the sun had risen well into the sky, but there were still deep shadows from the high wall that kept the training pool private and closed to public view. Beyond the wall she could hear visitors passing by, eager to see the elephants in their enclosure, gasping in surprise as they came across the rare mountain gorillas. A chair-lift whirred by, giving people a bird's eye view of the park. Further away, a giant water slide went into business; there were loud screams and a wild splash as the carriage hit the pool at the end of the ride. Life beyond the pool went on as normal.

Mandy sighed and leaned over the water to watch poor, sick Bob. He was swimming in slow circles, obviously looking for Bing. When he saw Mandy, he flipped his tail and rose to the surface.

'Hi!' She reached out to stroke him.

He hardly reacted. But he stayed close, taking in short bursts of air, still searching for his friend. He tilted his head towards her, as if to ask what they'd done with him.

'It's OK, he's safe in the big pool,' Mandy explained. 'We only took him away because you're sick. It won't be for long.' Her heart ached as the dolphin turned this way and that, gave a series of faint creaks, then gazed up at her again.

But Bob was so weak he could hardly move his flippers to stay afloat. His body dipped below the surface, then he struggled to rise.

And now Mandy began to be really afraid. Bob sucked in air, then sank. He rocked from side to side, unable to use his flippers to steady himself. He was sinking, then feebly trying to rise with a desperate flick of his broad tail.

Mandy stood up and looked around. Bob needed help, and she was certain that he needed it right now.

'Mel!' she cried. She heard someone come

in through the tall gate. 'Come quick!'

But it was Joel. He ran to her side. 'I just saw Mel in the office, talking to Mr Boston. What's wrong?'

'Oh, Joel, it's Bob. I think he's dying!'

He knelt to look. The dolphin could only just make it to the surface.

'If Matt Greenaway doesn't get here soon, he's going to be too late!'

'He needs air.' Joel acted quickly. He slipped into the water and tried to hold Bob up. 'Run and fetch Mel,' he called.

But Mandy couldn't leave them. 'Joel, he's saying goodbye. I know he is!'

Bob was nodding his head slowly, gasping and rolling in the water. And for all his effort, Joel was failing to hold him steady. In the end, he had to let him go.

Then the dolphin was free to float. He was making no movement, his blowhole was relaxing and letting in water. His eyes were closing for the last time.

Mandy watched the dolphin die. His lungs took in liquid. He dropped below the surface. Slowly, slowly the clear water met over his beautiful head and he sank to the bottom of the pool.

Mel sent word to Matt Greenaway that it was too late; Bob was dead.

'I can't believe it,' Mandy whispered to Joel. She felt crushed. 'I knew he was really sick, but I never thought he'd actually die.'

Joel stood by the side of the pool with her, watching them lift the body from the water. Bob had been so graceful, friendly and full of life. 'Me neither.'

'It's awful to think how he must have suffered.'

'Don't, Mandy. It's bad enough.' He walked away, his head hanging, unable to talk.

If only they could go back in time, just an hour, even half an hour, to when he was still alive! Mandy wished for the impossible. *Maybe I could have done something to save him!*

But it was too late. She too hung her head, and began to cry.

Lauren came and put an arm around her shoulders. 'It's tough,' she whispered. 'But we've still got work to do. I have to send samples to the lab in Orlando for tests to be done. We may never know what killed him,' she told Mandy, 'or maybe they'll find a virus. The important thing is making sure Bing stays well. Let's wait and see.'

It was early the following day, and everyone was slowly coming round from the shock. Outside the dolphinarium, life at Ibis Gardens still went on as usual.

'. . . So, we can go ahead with one dolphin,' Will Boston declared. 'Change the routines here and there, so that Bing takes over the tricks that Bob used to do. He can shoot a ball into a basket, can't he?'

Mandy shuddered. She stared at the theme park owner. Less than twenty-four hours after Bob had died, and Mr Boston was acting as if he couldn't care less. She still felt empty inside, and stunned.

And she sensed that Bing knew what had happened too. He'd swum restlessly near the surface for hours after Bob had died and been taken away, as if he'd been calling for him, longing for a reply.

Mel stood by the training pool shaking his head. 'I can't do that to him,' he argued.

'Why not? You know what they say – the show must go on.' Boston pointed at Bing, now swimming in slow circles deep below the surface. 'We still have a solo act here. And I can ship in another couple of dolphins for you to train up to join the show in a few weeks' time. What's the problem?'

Mandy could hardly bear to listen. Instead, she slipped her hand into the fish box and tempted Bing to the surface. She petted him and tried to comfort him as the two men talked on.

'The problem is, Bing here is pretty cut up about Bob dying.'

We all are, Mandy thought.

'You can't just go on as if nothing happened,' Mel insisted. 'Dolphins aren't machines. They're complex beings with highly developed intelligence and deep feelings!' His speech came from the heart as he looked his boss straight in the eye.

Boston shrugged. 'Yeah, well don't forget they pay your salary! And mine, and everyone's on the site. The dolphin show is what keeps this theme park going!'

Mandy stroked Bing's head and whispered to Joel. 'Let's jump in and keep him company.' Together they slipped into the water to swim beside the surviving dolphin.

Mel shook his head at Boston. 'This dolphin isn't fit to do the show, OK? How can I make this any easier for you? He just lost his lifetime companion. He doesn't know what hit him. It's called grief. He's lonely. I'm not gonna ask him to perform!' His face was red with a deep anger, his voice rising.

As Mandy and Joel swam alongside Bing, they knew that every word Mel said was true. Bing came close to them for contact, and still seemed to be looking everywhere for his missing friend.

Will Boston narrowed his eyes. He took a step back, then held his own. 'Lonely!' he retorted. 'You're crazy. You're telling me a dolphin thinks like a person?' There was a sneer on his broad face as he came to squat by the side of the pool. He watched Mandy and Joel swimming with Bing.

'So he can talk and tell you how he's feeling, can he?' he taunted.

'He doesn't have to.' Mandy couldn't help answering back. 'You can tell by the way he's acting.'

'He won't eat the fish, see.' Joel tried to add his opinion to the argument. 'And he won't play. Right now he should be rolling over and swimming under us, ducking and diving, fooling around. He hasn't done any of that since yesterday.' They'd brought him back into the training pool after Bob had been taken away, and he'd carried on calling and looking for him in vain.

'He's not sick too, is he?' Will Boston went into a panic. 'You say he's lost his appetite?'

Mel nodded, ready to make a stand. 'He needs better quality fish. I already ordered it from the supplier.'

Boston gritted his teeth, but for once didn't

complain. 'Has he got this fever, the same as the other one?'

'No. His temperature's normal,' Mel assured him. 'Whatever was wrong with Bob, Bing hasn't come down with it yet. It's like I said, he needs a better diet to build up his strength, especially now he's pining for his friend.'

Mr Boston stood up with the air of a man who had no more time to waste. 'So, take his mind off it, put him back to work,' he said abruptly. 'How soon can you get him ready?'

They might as well not have bothered, Mandy realised. She slipped her arm around Bing and stroked him on his nose.

Mel couldn't give any answer. He bit his lip and sighed.

'Put it this way, you've got until Friday.' Will Boston was on his way to the gate, striding off without looking back. 'Teach him the new tricks. Oh, and keep the kid in!'

From the far side of the pool Mandy glared at his disappearing back. Her eyes flashed. 'What if the kid doesn't want to stay in?' she muttered under her breath.

The gate slammed. Bing f licked his tail and dived out of sight.

'And what if the dolphin says no?' Joel said through clenched teeth.

Seven

'Bing's gone on strike,' Mandy told Jerry Logan. Joel's grandfather had driven over from Pelican's Roost to see how everyone was. It was Wednesday morning and it was growing clear that the surviving dolphin was desperately unhappy. He lurked at the bottom of the pool, refusing to do any of his tricks, coming up only for air.

'You gotta see his point of view,' Jerry admitted. 'He's already lost his mother, and now his brother. How would any of us feel if we lost someone special twice in such a short time?' With his wife, Bee, away in England he knew what it was like to feel lonely.

He turned to Steve Peratinos, who'd been brought in to give his advice.

The fisherman and the Green Earth gardener were old friends. They'd both lived on Blue Bayous all their lives and cared about nature and wildlife more than the likes of Will Boston. The theme park owner was a businessman and a newcomer as far as they were concerned. So they stood at the poolside with serious faces, watching the solitary dolphin.

'Can you think of anything that would help?' Mel asked. He'd racked his brains to find ways of cheering Bing up. 'I need to get him back in action, or else I'll have my boss on my back. But Bing doesn't want to know.' He pointed to a couple of coloured balls that bobbed on the surface. The dolphin had ignored them all morning.

Steve shrugged. 'The only thing that's gonna help this guy is the passage of time,' he murmured.

'Time is what we haven't got. Will's given me till the end of the week.'

Mandy had seen the posters by the main gate: 'Dolphin Shows Four Times a Day. Resumes Friday.'

'Bad news,' Steve tutted. 'I've seen a dolphin take

weeks to get over something like this. And that's out in the ocean where there's a whole school of them to help him cope.'

'Something like what?' Mandy was curious.

'Like, a young dolphin can lose his mother, say in an accident with a tuna net.'

'I thought they were against the law?' The big nets had been banned because of the damage they did to other sea creatures.

'Sure. But you get these big fishing companies. They think they're above the law. So once in a while, a mother dolphin gets killed. At Dolphin Watch we can put a tag on the young one and track him. You find he comes up to small boats, looking for the dead mother, maybe thinking the boat's a strange sort of dolphin; that it'll adopt him.'

Mandy sighed. 'Poor thing. So then what happens?'

'In the end he gives in and joins up with the nearest pod. But it takes him a few weeks to accept that the mother's gone. He seems to need someone special, and who can blame him?'

'Mel, *you're* special to Bing,' Mandy pointed out.

It seemed strange that the dolphin had turned his back on his trainer.

He frowned. 'I thought I was,' he said slowly. 'Now I'm not so sure.' He gazed down at Bing, then at the balls floating uselessly on the surface. 'Bing did trust me, but I kind of get the idea that he thinks I let him down.' His voice fell away, dejected.

'No, you didn't!' Mandy objected. She knew Mel cared more about the dolphins than anyone else.

'I was the one to take him away from Bob when he was dying. That can't look so good to him.'

Steve stepped in to reassure him. 'He'll come round. It's too soon right now. Like I said, he needs time.'

They'd come back to where they'd started. Time, as Mel said, was what they hadn't got.

Sadly the men moved off, leaving Mandy alone with Bing. They'd tried everything: changed Bing's diet, studied the results of the lab tests and asked advice from everyone they knew. Nothing had given them a clue about what to do for the best.

'Oh Bing, what can we do?' Mandy sighed, sitting to dangle her feet in the pool. She felt the sun on her back, and could hear the hum of visitors, the whirr of the cable cars.

'I've got an idea,' a voice said out of the blue.

She turned to see Joel, his cap perched on the back of his head, his hand delving into the fish box. 'What are you doing?' She jumped up as little Mitch came scampering towards them. 'Who let him out?'

The sea otter's webbed feet flapped on the wet surface, his broad tail smacked the ground. He smelt fish.

'I did.' Joel grinned at her. 'I figure if anyone can solve Bing's problem, it's gotta be Mitch!'

The sea otter grabbed and swallowed the fish, then plunged into the water. He darted to the far side of the pool and hopped out, spied Bing and dived in again; a dark, streamlined shape swimming close to the dolphin's head, inviting him to play.

Bing let Mitch say hello, then turned away. He swam slowly down the length of the pool.

Mitch shot to the surface and popped his broad head out of the water, his whiskers dripping, his large brown eyes puzzled. Then he disappeared for a second attempt. He raced after Bing and caught up with him, twisted underneath and came up the other side.

Joel and Mandy watched the two wavy shapes; one small and dark, the other large and shadowy. As they saw Bing ignore the sea otter's games, their hearts began to sink.

'Come on, Bing, play with Mitch!' Mandy breathed. She was on her hands and knees, craning out over the water.

Joel frowned. 'If Mitch can't help him, nothing can!'

But Bing was still too sad about Bob to take any notice of the lively little sea otter. Yet again he turned away.

Joel threw him another scrap of fish. 'Hey, look!' he whispered as the dolphin followed Mitch slowly to the surface. For a moment, they thought it had worked.

Mandy dug deep into the box for a fish to reward him with. Surely now Bing would come and feed, get over what had happened and let them coax him with treats. Mitch hopped out of the water and gave a short, pleased bark. Mandy held the fish at arm's length, tempting Bing to snatch it.

But the dolphin had only come up for oxygen. He rose like a submarine until his back broke the surface and he took in air. There was a wash of water against the side of the pool, a splash as his tail hit the surface. Then down he went, ignoring Mandy's fish, turning his back on his friends.

'No good.' Joel had to admit defeat. He scooped Mitch into his arms and stood there, head hanging, disappointed that his plan hadn't worked.

'You know what?' Mandy shook her head, recalling what Steve Peratinos had told them about dolphins getting better more quickly in the company of others. 'I think Bing is going to get so lonely here without Bob he could die!'

'No way.' Joel didn't want to hear this. He made off with Mitch, to put him back in his hutch.

Mandy ran after him. 'No, listen; he won't eat, he won't follow Mel's signals with the whistle. What I'm saying is, he won't take an interest in anything that's going on.' She paused. They stood by the gate, looking back at the pool. Bing had dived to the bottom and the water was still.

'So? It doesn't mean he's gonna die!'

'Of a broken heart,' Mandy said quietly. 'Don't you believe in that?'

Joel looked away. 'I guess. So what are you saying?' Mitch was squirming and wriggling over his shoulder, so he walked on with him, letting Mandy follow.

'I don't know!' Her thoughts were confused. Then she went back to what the fisherman had said. 'Joel, what would happen if we put Bing back into the ocean to be with other dolphins again? You know, like Steve said about the orphan dolphins. They look to the others to help them. Bing would do the same if we gave him the chance!'

'Put him back?' Joel repeated. He stared at her as if she'd gone crazy. 'How? How do you get a great big dolphin from the middle of an amusement park to the Gulf of Mexico?'

'I don't know how!' She hadn't thought this far. 'But what do you think? Would it work?'

Joel had opened Mitch's cage and put him back inside. The sea otter scuttled up and down, then sank his broad front teeth into a gnawed branch in the corner and chewed at it. 'To set him free?' He turned to her, jamming his cap over his forehead.

'Let's get this straight. You want Mel to ask Mr Boston if he's ready to let Bing go?'

Mandy nodded.

'For nothing?'

'Yes. Why not?'

'Do you know how much this dolphin's worth?'

'No. But whatever Bing's worth in money, you can't keep him cooped up here to pine away and die!'

'Thousands of dollars. Big bucks. Boston keeps telling us Ibis Gardens is short of money, remember. He isn't going to kiss goodbye to his star attraction!'

Mandy hesitated. Even she could see the point. 'What if we got someone to pay Mr Boston the money Bing is worth? Then he'd have to sell him.'

'Who?'

'I don't know. Lauren might have enough money at the rescue centre.'

'No way. They always need more money to look after the birds and animals they rescue.' Joel was definite about this. 'Gran works there for nothing because they can't afford to pay her.'

'OK, then; Steve Peratinos and Dolphin Watch.

They might be able to buy Bing and release him.' She trailed off as Joel shook his head once again. 'OK; the Millers next door to us at Pelican's Roost. They've got loads of money.'

'Mandy!' Joel spread his hands. 'Aren't you forgetting something?'

'What?'

'Even if we could raise the money somehow, we'd still have to get Mel on our side.'

She paused. Yes, she'd been racing ahead as usual. 'OK, so it would be a hard choice for him. I know that.'

'Like, he's worked with Bing since he was born. And he's already lost Bob.' They were walking down one of the main paths through the park, against the steady flow of visitors which was filing in through the gates. 'Think how it would feel if he had to say goodbye to Bing as well.'

'Terrible,' Mandy admitted. 'But, like I say, it would be even worse if Bing stays here and pines away.'

'Who's pining away?' Mel himself came cutting through the crowd towards them. He'd just seen Steve Peratinos and Jerry Logan off and was hurrying back to the dolphinarium. 'You mean Bing, don't you? How is he?'

'Not good,' Joel admitted. He told him about Mitch's failed attempt to cheer him up.

Mel listened in silence. 'OK, and let me guess what you two were discussing.' He went and leaned on a wooden rail by the alligator compound. A couple of two-metre long specimens were lazing in the mud by the edge of the lake. One opened its wide gash of a mouth and showed them its rows of spiked teeth. 'You think we should get Bing out of here,' he said quietly.

Mandy gasped. 'How did you know?'

'Because it's pretty much what I figure too.' He was thinking hard, staring at his hands which he'd clasped together as he leaned his elbows on the rail.

The two alligators shifted into the water and sailed gently away. They looked like pieces of driftwood, except for the two pairs of gleaming yellow eyes.

'That we should set him free?' Mandy glanced at Joel with new hope.

Mel nodded. 'This latest disaster is the final straw,

as far as I'm concerned. After all, what kind of life does he have here now that Bob's gone?'

From the big island in the middle of the lake, a troupe of monkeys squealed and chattered at the approach of the alligators. They swung away through the trees.

'I've been thinking things through ever since Dorothy died last year. What right do we have to keep them in the first place? OK, so it's been my life. Training dolphins to do these shows, getting them to trust me. But I guess it's time to make changes.'

Joel broke the silence. 'So what now?'

The trainer stood up straight, as if he'd made his decision. 'Go to see the boss,' he told them. 'Get him to give Bing his life back.'

'Now?' Mandy asked.

There was firmness in his stride as he made his way to the office.

'Sure. Do you want to come?'

Mandy was there with him, her chin up, determined for Bing's sake that they would make Boston see sense.

'What if he says no?' Joel demanded. He ran ahead of them and started to walk backwards, begging them to think before they acted.

The office door was open. They could see the head and shoulders of the park owner as he sat at his desk.

'Don't worry, he'll say yes,' Mel told them, without a moment's hesitation.

'No way, no way, no way!' Will Boston slammed his desk drawer. 'You've seen the posters! We begin again Friday!'

Mandy could feel Mel trembling with anger. She didn't know how he kept his own temper as his boss flared up.

'We can't begin unless the dolphin is willing to perform,' he pointed out.

'What is this? You're telling me you can't train this animal to do the act?' Boston raged on. 'It's a dolphin, not a movie star!' he ranted.

'Bing's got a mind of his own, and if he's not ready to do it, there's nothing I can do.'

'You call yourself an animal trainer!'

Mandy saw Boston's dark moustache quiver. He'd turned them down flat; no way was he going to let Bing go free.

'Let me make it clear. We re-open Friday with one dolphin. I'm buying two more dolphins from Underwater World up in Star Bay. I've just called them. They can send a truck down tomorrow. The dolphins are fifteen months old.'

'That's too young,' Mel cut in. 'They're not fully weaned. The guys at Underwater World should know that!'

'Tough. When they get here, you start training. I'll give you two months to work them into the show. Think you can do it?' The question came out as a sneer as he walked right up to Mel and stuck his face out in a fresh challenge.

Mel measured his reply. 'OK, so if I train two new dolphins, does that mean that at the end of two months, I can take Bing and put him in the ocean?'

If he lives that long, Mandy thought. She felt her heart thumping inside her chest, she saw Joel shaking his head and looking down at his feet.

Will Boston laughed in Mel's face. 'Nice try. But like I said; no way!'

Mel jutted out his chin. For a second, Mandy thought he was going to take a swing at his boss.

Instead, he turned and headed for the door. 'Fine. I quit!' he yelled. 'I'm out of here!'

Stunned, she watched Will Boston's mouth fall open, heard him turn and thump his desk. Then she and Joel ran after Mel as fast as they could.

The porch lights were on at Pelican's Roost. Jerry Logan had invited a bunch of people over for the evening. There was Lauren Young from GRROWL, Steve Peratinos from Dixie Springs, and Mel Hartley himself. It was only hours since he'd quit his job at Ibis Gardens and he was already regretting his decision.

'You did the only thing you could,' Lauren told him. She was sipping a cool drink, looking out across the garden at the white beach beyond.

'But what happens now?' Mel had left Bing in the lurch. He'd stormed out of the office and straight out of the gate. Joel had only just been able to calm him down enough to drive over to his grandfather's house to explain what had taken place. Jerry had rung round and invited the others over for the evening.

'Let's just get our heads around this,' Steve said.

'Did you quit, or did Boston fire you?'

'I quit.'

'So change your mind. Give him a call, say you want your job back.'

Mel sank his head on to his chest.

'He doesn't,' Mandy explained. 'What we all want is for Mr Boston to let Bing go. We think it's his only chance since he's so miserable without Bob.'

'Wow! I'd say we have a big problem on our hands. What do we do now?' Steve asked.

'We can't steal a dolphin from under his nose, that's for sure!' Jerry Logan tried to make light of it. He went inside for more drinks, but somehow his words stuck in Mandy's head.

'Can't steal a dolphin!' They spun around inside her brain as Jerry served pizza and salad to go with the drinks. They stuck in her mind as they finished the meal and she took the plates inside to stack them in the dishwasher. 'Can't steal a dolphin?' Mandy gazed at her reflection in the dark window.

'I don't see why we can't steal a dolphin!' Mandy said to Joel as he brought more dishes into the kitchen.

'Uh-oh!' He caught the glint in her eye, the

stubborn note in her voice. 'No, don't tell me!' Joel backed away, raising both hands as she came towards him.

But Mandy grabbed him before he could escape. 'Come with me. I want to tell you something!' She took him to walk on the beach under the moon and stars.

'. . . Steal a dolphin?' he echoed.

'We need a big tank full of seawater and a truck. One of those giant trucks you see taking oranges to the factories on the mainland. Only instead of a

load of oranges, we would have Bing in the tank.'

The waves rose and crashed on to the shore. Moonlight glittered on the black sea.

'. . . We'd tell Mr Boston that Bing was sick.'

'Like Bob?'

'. . . Say he'd caught the virus. Mr Boston would have to believe us if Lauren gave him the news. She'd tell him that Bing needed to go to a dolphin clinic somewhere.'

'In Orlando?' Joel remembered that Matt Greenaway, the dolphin expert, worked there. Still he shook his head and walked barefoot along the beach. 'You're crazy!' he said.

'. . . Boston hears from Lauren that Bing needs urgent treatment. He has to let the truck come into Ibis Gardens to pick him up for the journey. Only, it's not Matt Greenaway's truck, it's us!'

'And we take him to Dixie Springs?' Joel was beginning to get the picture.

'To Steve and his Dolphin Watch people.' Mandy was so excited, she could hardly keep from running back to the house and spilling it out to the grown-ups. 'We get the tank down into the harbour and we set Bing free! He'll swim out to sea. Other dolphins will come to meet him . . . !'

'Mandy!' Joel warned. 'I'm not sure we should do it. I mean, we're breaking the law here!'

She nodded. 'I know. But if we don't, Bing is going to die. First his mother, then his brother. Are we prepared just to hang around and wait for it to happen to him too?' It wasn't just her; Mel thought the same way, and he was an expert.

'OK.' Joel considered it and agreed. 'But there's still a pretty big "if" in this before we even get near to putting your plan into action.'

'What?' Mandy couldn't see any flaws in her argument. And there was no time to lose. She was heading back up the beach over the soft, silvery sand.

'*If* we can get Lauren to help us,' he pointed out, running after her. 'We have to get her to tell a pretty big lie, remember!'

Mandy gulped. Joel was right. Was there any way Lauren would go along with their plan?

'It's a matter of life and death!' Mandy begged Lauren Young to listen to her. The grown-ups sat on the Logans' porch trying to decide what to do.

'We could go to jail for stealing.' Joel's grandpa wanted them to steady down. 'This is pretty big stuff!'

'But what else can we do?' By now Joel was firmly on Mandy's side. He'd had time to think about it since she broke the idea to him on the beach.

It was a question that no one could answer.

'Who says Will Boston will listen to me?' Lauren asked. 'He's had this fight with Mel here, and he knows Mel and I are good friends. Even if we did try Mandy's plan, I don't think he would trust me.'

They sat in their cane chairs, staring up at the stars. For a while no one spoke.

'So, who *would* he trust?' Joel wanted to know.

There was another silence. Slowly every head in the group turned towards Mandy.

'Me?' she yelped, jumping up in surprise. This was something she hadn't bargained for.

'Sure. You heard what he said: "Keep the kid in!" ' Joel insisted. 'He likes you!'

'He doesn't even know me!' All Will Boston knew was that she could do a good trick with his two dolphins. The crowd liked it, and whatever the crowd liked, Boston was in favour of.

'But you're the one who could persuade him to listen to Lauren.' Joel explained it slowly, refusing to let her back off. 'You could go in tomorrow like nothing had gone wrong, ready to work with Bing. Act all innocent!'

'Me?' Mandy was finding it hard to agree. 'But that means I'd have to be nice to Mr Boston!'

'You can do it. Think of what would happen to Bing if you don't.'

'So, she says she'll train Bing until the boss hires another helper?' Mel looked ahead. 'He says yes. She works for a couple of hours then goes back and tells him she's called Lauren to take another look at the dolphin because he's sick. That's when Lauren gives her verdict; Bing needs to go to the clinic in Orlando!'

'You got it!' Joel grinned at them. 'What do you say?'

Mandy stared at them in turn. Mel was nodding, Jerry was talking it through with Steve Peratinos.

Even Lauren agreed she would be willing to take the risk for Bing's sake. 'But it's down to you, Mandy,' she said quietly, fixing her with her calm, dark brown eyes.

Mandy took a deep breath. Even though it was her idea, she hadn't imagined playing this major role. It would be like acting a part in a play. Could she do it?

'Mandy?' Joel grew impatient. 'We gotta decide.'

'OK,' she said at last. 'I can't make any promises that I can pull this off, but I'll give it a go.'

Eight

'Hi, Mr Boston!' Mandy breezed into the office at Ibis Gardens early next morning. Joel and Jerry Logan had driven her across and wished her luck. They would wait in the car park for a while. Then, if all was well, they would drive on to meet Lauren and Mel at GRROWL. Meanwhile, Steve Peratinos had contacted his Dolphin Watch friends and they were on standby at Dixie Springs.

Will Boston was on the phone. He was worried and cross as usual, when he looked up and spotted Mandy. 'What? Oh, hi!'

He turned away to argue down the line. 'Listen,

you gotta take those two young dolphins back to Star Bay! I can't keep them here . . . I just lost my trainer, that's why! . . . No, I don't care if the truck's already set off. You call the driver and tell him I changed my mind!'

Mandy watched him slam down the phone. She felt the palms of her hands begin to sweat.

'Whadaya-want?' he snapped.

'I came to help with Bing,' Mandy said, all sweet and bright.

Boston's frown deepened. 'You know I fired Mel Hartley?'

She held his gaze. Not so much fired, as the other way round, she knew. But she said nothing. She hoped her innocent, bright-eyed stare would settle his suspicions.

'Yeah, you were there,' he recalled. 'So how come you still want to work with the dolphin?'

'I like him,' Mandy said simply. 'And he likes me.'

Boston sniffed and twitched his moustache. 'You think you can work with him alone until I get someone else?'

'I'd like to try.' She was doing OK, keeping a smile on her face, though her hands were hot and sticky now, and her mouth felt dry.

Boston shoved papers around on his desk and snatched up the phone once more. 'Mac, is that you? Get the 'copter out for me, will-ya? I gotta go to Miami to talk to my banker.' He glanced up at Mandy. 'Go ahead, what are you waiting for?' he snapped. No thanks, no grateful smile.

So Mandy slipped out before he could change his mind.

'Just don't let Mel Hartley get the idea that he can come crawling back!' he yelled after her. 'Tell him from me never to show his face, OK! Good trainers are a dime a dozen!' He punched more numbers into the phone, too proud to admit he was wrong.

Mandy was over the first hurdle and heading for the dolphinarium. It was only eight o'clock; too early for visitors to be allowed in the park. A few keepers dressed in green polo-shirts and fawn shorts were sweeping and mucking out in the animal compounds. They gave her a friendly wave.

She hurried on, glad to find the gate to the training pool unlocked, but afraid of how Bing would be after his second lonely night. Hoping he would at least be hungry, Mandy took a bucket of the new fish from the cold store.

Normally he would have come to the surface the moment Mel had blown the whistle. But this morning, like yesterday, it was different. Mandy blew twice, then three times. She could see the dolphin's shadowy shape settled in a corner, ignoring the high-pitched sound.

If Bing wouldn't come to her, she would go to him, Mandy decided. She dived in and swam underwater, greeting him with a fond pat. He gave a small response, lifting his head to let her tickle his flat chin, as if he still wanted to please her, then he rose with her to the surface.

'That's right!' Mandy encouraged. 'See, it's not so bad up here. I've brought some beautiful fish for your breakfast.' She talked on as she swam to fetch it, thinking that the sound of her voice would boost Bing's spirits. Her own hopes rose as he followed in her wake, making low creaking noises in reply. He was 'talking back' in his own way, trying his best to be friendly.

'Nice fresh fish,' she cooed, reaching into the bucket. 'Mel ordered it specially for you.'

But Bing veered away as she dangled it in front of his nose. He wasn't hungry.

Mandy sighed, then climbed out to try a game with him. If he wouldn't eat, maybe he would play. So she brought the blue ball and tossed it into the water. It landed with a splash. 'Come on, Bing, pass it to me!' She stood at the poolside, hands outstretched, waiting for him to flip it back with his beak.

Again she was disappointed. The dolphin swam up to the ball, then straight past, nosing it out of the way in a sad, empty manner. He disappeared to the far end of the pool.

What else could she try? Other noises to attract his attention. She rattled a pole against the metal fish bucket and waited. Nothing. Bing didn't move from the deepest part of the pool. She even sang a song about sailing across the sea, sailing home, sailing to be free.

She sang the words from the bottom of her heart, willing the dolphin to shake off his grief and listen. But he'd been too badly affected by Bob's death to respond.

'Oh Bing, my singing can't be that bad!' Mandy

pleaded. It hurt her to see him like this – so sad and lonely. Was this the same dolphin who had played tricks on people and fooled around to please the crowds? It was hard to believe as she peered into the pool and saw him barely moving, his face turned to the wall.

Something had to be done. It was time to put the next stage of their plan into action.

'Don't worry, we're going to get help,' Mandy promised him. She got up from her hands and knees and went to use the public phone beside the main gate. 'Lauren, can you come?' she said quickly.

'I'm on my way!' she promised. 'Give me twenty minutes.'

Just time to tell her that all was going according to plan so far. 'Mr Boston doesn't suspect a thing!' she whispered into the phone. Then she hung up and went to walk by the lake until Lauren showed up.

Mandy's nerves were stretched to breaking point as she waited. Twice she went out into the car park to see if the GRROWL truck had arrived, twice she went to phone Joel and ask him to make sure that everyone was standing by.

Then, when Lauren did make it after only fifteen minutes, they both hurried straight to Will Boston's office.

'What now?' He was already at the door, looking at his watch. When he saw Mandy and Lauren, he made it clear that he had no time to spare.

'I got Lauren to look at Bing because he wouldn't do any work with me,' Mandy explained hurriedly. 'She says now he's fallen sick too.'

'What kind of sick? Not this fever that killed the other two? That's just what we need!' Worried and angry, the boss went to the phone and gave orders. 'Mac? Where's the 'copter? I told you to get it here five minutes ago!' He clicked the switch and tore into Mandy and Lauren. 'Come on, give it to me straight. Is he gonna die?'

'Maybe.' Lauren wouldn't be definite.

So far she hadn't even had to lie, Mandy realised. Instead, she'd let Boston jump to his own conclusions.

'I got a lot of money tied up in that dolphin,' Boston reminded her. 'What can you do to save him?' As always, it was money that came first.

'He needs treatment. I can't give it to him here.

I'd like to take him to Matt Greenaway in Orlando. He's the best dolphin man in the state.'

Here came the lie. Mandy watched Lauren grit her teeth and drop her gaze. Luckily Boston was too busy to notice.

'Can't you get the guy to come down here?'

'Not fast enough. You want me to go ahead?'

'How much will it cost me?'

'Not a cent.'

Lauren's promise stopped Boston in his tracks. 'You can get your rescue centre to pay for the treatment? How about the transportation?'

'The people from Dolphin Watch are going to provide a truck.'

This was true, Mandy knew. Steve Peratinos had friends who owned a big truck. And Dolphin Watch could put their hands on a suitable tank to transport Bing out of Ibis Gardens. It was all laid on.

The idea of free treatment to solve a serious situation was too much for Boston to resist. Besides, the noisy grind and whirr of a helicopter's blades sounded overhead. He considered the proposal, glanced once in Mandy's direction, then nodded his head. 'Go ahead,' he grunted.

Mandy felt her heart lurch as the helicopter landed on the pad behind the office. Its blades slowed and clattered noisily, drowning her muttered thanks.

'Let's go!' Lauren yelled above the machine's roar.

As Will Boston jammed his hat on his head, ducked low to avoid the wind from the blades and clambered aboard his private helicopter, Mandy and Lauren went into the next stage of the plan.

Getting Bing out of Ibis Gardens went like clockwork. Steve Peratinos was at the gate with the truck before half past nine. Jerry Logan and Joel sat in the high cab with him, ready to help lower the crate containing the special tank to take the dolphin away.

Mandy and Lauren had already dealt with the other Ibis Gardens keepers, telling them the same story that Lauren had told Will. So the gate opened for the truck and it drove slowly in.

Mandy ran alongside as it chugged towards the dolphinarium. She gave Joel a thumbs-up sign. So far, so good.

'Mel's here!' he mouthed down at her, pointing

to the sleeping-compartment above his head. 'Just in case we need him.'

'Don't let anyone see him!' The news that he'd quit had spread like wildfire. He mustn't be spotted now.

But Mandy was glad Mel was there when they finally backed the truck up to the gates of the training pool and he could get out of the cab without being seen. As Steve and the others got the tank into position and began to lower it into the pool with a pulley and chains, she spoke anxiously to him.

'I don't know how we're going to persuade Bing to do this,' she admitted. 'I can't get him to obey any orders at all. You'll have to see if you can!'

Mel nodded. He took a look into the pool. 'Poor guy, he must wonder what's going on here.'

The plastic tank had hit the water with a splash. Beneath the ripples and broken surface they could see Bing huddled in a corner.

'If you can get him to come up and say hi, I'll get ready with a shot of tranquilliser,' Lauren told them. 'He'll still be conscious and breathing, but it'll make the journey easier for him if he's sedated.'

'*If* I can get him to say hi!' Mel looked unhappy. He took a whistle from his pocket and blew a familiar signal. 'He's not gonna forgive me for this!'

Mandy watched Bing hear the sound and suddenly flick his tail so that he was pointing upwards. He seemed to be looking for Mel, waiting for another signal.

The trainer blew again and the dolphin came swimming slowly to the surface.

'He'll forgive you when he realises why you're doing it,' Mandy reminded him. It was hard when an animal trusted you and it looked as if you were letting him down.

She could hardly bear to look as Bing broke the surface and spotted Mel. He rattled out a message and rolled in the water, almost like his old self.

'Hi, Bing!' Mel reached out to him. 'Did you think I'd gone and left you on your own?'

The dolphin was too busy greeting Mel to notice Lauren come alongside with her syringe full of tranquilliser. But he felt the jab. Too late, he turned away. The drug took rapid effect and within seconds Bing was wallowing weakly in the water.

'Let's go!' The vet gave the order.

Mel, Mandy and Joel jumped into the pool. They got underneath Bing and supported him as the men in the truck manoeuvred the tank by pulling levers inside the cab. Slowly they edged it into position.

Then, when the time was right, Mel, Joel and Mandy nudged Bing into the tank. He was too dazed to resist, so Mel could give the signal for the tank to be lifted with the dolphin inside it.

Mandy saw the tank move skywards. The chains took the strain of a tank full of water and dolphin. A metal arm swung the load sideways. Soon it was lodged firmly on the back of the huge truck.

And before they knew it, Steve had slotted the crate into place around it. He and Jerry Logan made everything secure, then climbed into the cab.

'Everyone stand clear!' Jerry yelled, ordering Mel and Joel back into the truck.

Lauren nodded at Mandy. 'You did a good job.'

'Thanks, but it's not over yet. Tell me that when we get Bing to Dixie Springs!' Mandy ran for the car with Lauren. 'Come on, let's lead the way!'

The truck was on the move with its live cargo. No one suspected a thing.

Nine

Mandy sat next to Lauren as they drove out of the main gates at Ibis Gardens. On the road behind, towering over them, Steve Peratinos was at the wheel of the gleaming silver truck.

They had got Bing clear of the theme park. Now they took the north road to Dixie Springs. Mandy heaved a sigh of relief and signalled to Joel, who sat between his grandfather and Steve in the cab. Behind them, tucked away in the sleeping-compartment, Mel was once more in hiding.

Joel waved back.

They were on the move; it was really happening.

They were going to take the lonely dolphin to the sea and set him free! Mandy grinned at Lauren, then hung on to the rollbar as the truck braked for a posse of cyclists heading for a nearby beach. Their striped towels were strapped to their bikes, they wore beach bags across their shoulders, and they were in no hurry to get out of the way.

'Come on!' Lauren tapped the steering-wheel.

As the road cleared, she put her foot down and they were off again, past ranch-style luxury homes overlooking the beach, across white bridges built over the narrow straits. The road ran on concrete pillars over the deep blue sea. To either side Mandy could see small fishing boats and leisure cruisers, while straight ahead the road ran smooth and broad. Looking over her shoulder, she could see Bing's truck following without trouble.

'That marina over there is Captiva Harbour.' Lauren pointed out a cluster of white buildings next to a small harbour. 'The next one up is Dixie!'

After the bridge, the road curved inland. They drove between tall palm trees with graceful, feathery leaves, through patches of shade where mangrove trees grew in salt water swamps. Mandy held on to the bar as the truck swayed and the road took a curve back towards the sea. The water sparkled in the sunlight, and there, across the next bay, was the sponge fishing village of Dixie Springs.

Bing was only minutes away from freedom when Lauren picked up her car phone to answer a call. Mandy saw her stiffen as she listened to the voice on the end of the line.

'It's Will Boston!' she whispered. 'He says he's coming after us!' She slammed down the phone and gripped the wheel. Ahead of them lay a bridge across the final bay.

'How come?' Mandy leaned out of the window and strained to see what was coming up behind the truck.

'Not by road – by 'copter!' Lauren told her. 'He was on his way to Miami and he phoned Matt Greenaway to ask him if he knew whether Bing was safely on his way.'

'Oh no!' Mandy felt her stomach churn. 'And Matt told him he knew nothing about it?'

Lauren nodded. 'Right. Boston's gone crazy. He must have guessed what we were trying to do. He's been calling everyone to get hold of my mobile number and now he's managed to find out where we are and is heading back this way!'

Mandy looked up into the blue sky. There was only a jet flying high above the earth, streaming its white trail of exhaust. No helicopter, not yet. But she thought she could hear something above the roar of the truck's engine as it trundled close behind them on to the bridge. The sound was harsh and mechanical. And then she saw a helicopter lurch into view.

'What are we going to do?' Mandy's hair streamed back from her face in the wind as she craned to see.

Lauren didn't answer. She kept her foot on the accelerator and got on the phone to Steve. Looking over her shoulder, Mandy saw him pick his phone up and speak into it, and saw Joel's reaction as he heard the news. She watched him shoot his head out of the window to catch sight of the helicopter, and saw his face go pale as he turned to look at her.

Mandy still hung out of the window. The sound of the helicopter's blades grew louder. The machine was catching up, hovering almost overhead. 'What now?' she yelled above the roar.

'Keep going!' Joel cried back. 'We can still do it!'

She read his lips. 'Joel says, keep going,' she gasped at Lauren. At least they all knew that Boston was on their trail. There was no mistaking it now. Above their heads, the helicopter dipped and rocked unsteadily, its blades slicing through the air as it tried to move in even closer. Through the glass dome of the cockpit Mandy could see two figures. The one at the controls must be Boston's driver, Mac, while Boston himself was leaning forward and waving his arms at them.

'Doesn't he know that his 'copter will scare Bing half to death?' Lauren frowned. Its shadow fell across the tank on the back of the truck. The noise and the sight would terrify the already frightened dolphin.

'He doesn't care.' In Mandy's mind, Will Boston cared much more about money than he did about animals. He pretended to do what was best, but he was too worried about his business being in debt to really look after them. 'He wants Bing back and he doesn't care how he does it!'

'We're never gonna shake him off,' Lauren told Mandy. She was driving as fast as she dared, keeping an eye on the overhead mirror to make sure that the truck could keep up with her. But however fast she went, the helicopter still lurched overhead. Other cars on the bridge were braking and pulling into the side of the road to watch the chase.

Then Boston came back on the phone. This time Mandy picked it up. She heard him yell at them to stop, throwing threats around about what he would do.

'If you're doing what I think you're doing and planning to put that dolphin back in the sea, I'll sue you all! That Rescue Centre won't have a cent to its name when I'm through! This is theft, plain and simple!'

'Listen, Mr Boston,' Mandy pleaded. 'Just listen for a moment!'

'Like heck I will! You tell Jerry Logan I'll wipe him out. I'll take him to court and ruin him and his gardening business! *And* that Dolphin Watch!'

'But Bing will die if you keep him at Ibis Gardens!' Mandy grabbed the bar as Lauren swung off the bridge on to a narrow road signposted to Dixie Springs. Behind them, the nearside wheels of the huge truck left the road and churned up a thick cloud of sandy soil. After a few seconds Steve got control again and managed to follow. Mandy could see that up in the cab Mel Hartley had come out of hiding and was hanging on to the back of Joel's seat.

'I said stop!' The cloud of dust rose and swirled around the helicopter as Boston carried on shouting.

'Forget it,' Lauren muttered to Mandy, her hands still gripping the wheel. 'He's not gonna listen to reason.'

So Mandy switched the phone off. The rising cloud of dust had given her a faint hope that they could keep the helicopter at bay while they went ahead with their plan. She explained a new idea to Lauren. 'Don't drive down to the harbour. That's where the road goes right down to the water, isn't it?'

Lauren braked and nodded. 'For trailers to take boats down.'

'Right. So we lead the truck away from that ramp and along the beach instead.'

'What for?' Lauren had to make a decision. Whichever way she went, the truck would follow.

'Because by driving along the beach, the wheels of the truck will churn up all the dry sand, like that soil at the side of the road back there!' She waited for Lauren to understand. 'We'll make a kind of sand storm, so the helicopter can't follow us!'

'Good thinking!' Lauren made up her mind and swerved away from the small quay. Instead, she led Steve across a patch of spiky, rough grass that led on to the beach itself. 'If we can keep them at a distance and force them to land away from where we stop, we might have time to lower the tank and get Bing safely into the water!'

Mandy hung on tight. Over her shoulder she could see the four of them in the cab wondering whether they should follow. She nodded and waved them on, praying that they would understand.

'Are they coming?' Lauren's wheels had hit the beach and begun to churn up dust. She struggled to get a grip.

'Yep.' Mandy turned to face the front. Ahead lay a long stretch of empty white sand. 'This has got to work!' she muttered. She hoped that the beach would be firm enough to let them drive, yet loose enough for the wheels to kick up the dust cloud.

'Yes!' she cried, as Lauren's wheels bit and they moved on.

Now for Steve's truck. Its giant wheels sank into the sand, its engine whined, the wheels began to spin. Then the thick tread on the tyres took hold. Slowly it inched its way on to the beach.

Above their heads, the helicopter whirled in small circles. It clung like a giant insect to their backs, until the huge truck sent up a gritty cloud of dry sand. As it rose towards them, the pilot clutched at the controls and suddenly veered away, rising higher into the sky, waiting for the cloud to settle.

'It's working!' Mandy told Lauren. 'Let's go!' The faster they drove, the bigger the sandstorm. She waved Steve on towards the shoreline.

But they only had minutes. Soon Mac would rise above the dusty barrier. He might decide to steer around it and approach from the other side. Or he could land at a safe distance. Meanwhile, they had to unload the tank and set Bing free.

So they raced along the beach until the churning storm of dry sand had risen and blocked out the tiny, clean houses at the harbourside. Now, though they could hear Boston's helicopter, it was hidden from view.

'How about now? Should we try?' Lauren asked.

Mandy nodded, then hung on as she swung towards the white waves at the edge of the clear sea. Once more Steve followed.

They reached the waves and drove in, axle-deep. Then they jumped to the ground and ran to help the others slide the tank into position so that it could be lowered on a hydraulic lift at the tail of the truck. They worked in a haze of gritty sand that had begun to settle as soon as the trucks had come to a standstill.

'Make it go faster!' Joel called to Steve, as the platform lowered the tank slowly into the shallow waves.

'This is as fast as it goes!' he cried back.

Somewhere, not too far away, the helicopter hovered; heard but hidden from view.

'That's good!' Mandy whispered, keeping her fingers crossed. For as long as the dust cloud stayed in the air, they could keep Boston guessing.

At last the tank hit the ground with a thump. Water splashed and spilled over the edges, as

Mandy, Joel and Mel waded into the sea up to their knees.

'Did you hear that?' Jerry Logan called from dry land. He stood with one hand to his forehead, shielding his eyes from the flying sand. 'The 'copter's landed!'

Mandy paused to listen. It was true; the noisy engine had cut out, the blades whirred and slowed. 'How do we open this thing?' she urged Mel.

It was still impossible to see beyond the cloud, but they could be sure that Will Boston had landed some distance away, had clambered to the ground, and at this very minute was running as fast as he could towards them.

Mel showed them how to unbolt a sealed, sliding gate at one end of the tank. Inside, through the opaque plastic sides, they could make out Bing's shadowy shape. He was alert, nosing at the sides of the tank, already over the effects of the mild tranquilliser.

'When we slide this, the water rushes out and the dolphin comes with it,' Mel warned. 'Ready?'

Mandy swallowed hard. There was a band of fear around her chest, making it difficult to breathe.

The helicopter blades had finally died and left a huge silence. Then there were footsteps, thudding along the sand, splashing into the shallow waves at the water's edge.

'OK!' she gasped.

Mel unlocked the final bolt. They shoved the gate aside . . . and Bing slid into the sea on a torrent of released water.

Ten

'Swim!' Mandy cried. She stood knee deep in the sea, urging him on.

The dolphin lay on the shore. A wave rolled and crashed against him.

'Quickly, before Mr Boston gets here!'

His footsteps came splashing along the shore. He was shouting at them to stop.

Bing was stranded in shallow water, helpless.

'We've got to get him in deeper!' There was panic in Mandy's voice. Bing thrashed with his tail, seeming to recognise what was happening. Could he hear some high-pitched signals from fellow dolphins further out to sea? Their plan was so near to success, yet so far away.

Meanwhile, Boston fought his way through the soft, wet sand towards them. 'Come on, Mac. We gotta stop this fool thing!'

Mandy could see his stooped figure emerging through the dust. 'Bing!' she pleaded. She ran deeper into the sea, urging him on. A strong wave broke against her, almost knocking her off her feet.

Bing tried to follow. Water washed around him, almost lifting his belly clear of the sloping beach. But as the wave crashed and ebbed, he was left struggling on dry land again.

'Next time we get a big wave, we'll lift him and let him float out on it!' Mandy cried. She had one hand on Bing's broad back, one under his belly, ready to act.

Joel ran round to the far side, kicking up water, stumbling in the drag of the current. 'Come on!' He urged the next wave to swell and crash against the shore.

'No, you don't!' Boston lunged towards them, followed by his helicopter pilot.

Jerry Logan stepped into his path. 'I'll handle

this,' he told Steve and Lauren. 'You help the kids.'

So they came and helped Joel and Mandy to take the dolphin's weight, laying gentle hands on him as they saw the next swelling wave, the first fringe of white foam as it began to break.

'Wait!' Mandy wanted the moment to be right. 'OK, Bing, when we lift you, you've got to swim!'

The salt air filled his lungs. He scented freedom.

'Watch this!' Jerry refused to let Boston pass. The theme park boss tried to dodge sideways, but it was too late.

The wave broke with a crash. The force of the water lifted Bing, and five pairs of helping hands guided him out of danger, into deep water.

'Swim!' Mandy and Joel whispered together. They launched him gently, praying for him to use his flippers and powerful tail.

'There you go!' Mel stood up straight. 'We've done all we can. It's down to you.'

Would Bing seize his chance?

His head went back. He was listening. Time seemed to stand still as he heard the dolphins of Dixie Springs call from the wild.

Mandy couldn't see them or hear them, but she knew they were there.

Bing glanced back at Mel. He half wanted to stay. But the lure of the deep was too strong. With a flick of his tail he launched himself out to sea.

'Fabulous!' Joel sighed.

Bing was swimming, pushing through the foam with strong strokes. Mandy swam alongside him, urging him on.

And there, gathered close to the shore, was a whole school of dolphins waiting for Bing. Sunlight glistened on the sea, breaking the surface into a million golden ripples.

Mandy felt Bing break away from her. He answered the wild dolphins, then vanished below the water.

'Goodbye!' she said out loud. A stream of bubbles burst around her as Bing dived.

She thought it was over: Will Boston standing with Jerry Logan on the beach, watching his dolphin strike out into the ocean, Mel, Steve, Joel and Lauren bunched together on the shoreline, the wild dolphins calling.

But then the most amazing thing happened.

Mandy felt the water swirl under her, found herself lifted from below. Her arms shot into the air as she struggled for balance, then she knew she was astride Bing. He was rising to the surface with her on his back. He was carrying her out to sea!

For a split second Mandy was scared. What if he took her way out into the deep? He was speeding out of the bay towards his new friends, who came to swim alongside them, leaping and tumbling in welcome. How would she ever get back to the shore?

She heard Joel shout and Mel whistle. But no: now she wasn't frightened. Bing wouldn't harm her. She sat safely astride his back, her arms raised in joy and delight as they sped through the water. She was riding a dolphin. It was exciting, thrilling, brilliant . . . magical!

Bing swept across the bay with Mandy on his back. He brought her full-circle towards the shore.

It was over. This was really goodbye.

Gently he let her down a few metres from her friends. He left her floating in shallow water and swam away again to join the school of wild dolphins. She didn't want to watch him swim away this last time. Knowing that he was safe was enough.

So she swam until her feet touched the bottom, then she waded out of the water. Tears mixed with the salt sea on her wet cheeks, as Lauren came towards her and put her arms around her.

'He's happy,' the vet whispered.

'So am I.' Mandy wiped her face. She looked up at Joel and smiled.

He nodded and grinned back.

'Listen,' Jerry Logan told them, beckoning them all on to dry land. 'Will's just had a great idea!'

Will? Mandy pulled a face. Why wasn't Mr Boston yelling at them for letting Bing go? Why was he standing there with a new look on his face? Was that a smile beneath his dark moustache?

'Tell them!' Joel's grandfather encouraged him.

They gathered round under the hot sun.

'It came to me when I saw that trick you just did!' he told Mandy.

'That was no . . . trick!' That was one hundred per cent Bing saying thank you for giving him his freedom. She was about to explain to Boston when Joel dug his elbow into her arm.

'Great! Really great. So I'm standing here

watching the trick, and it hits me: a unique new dolphin experience for visitors to Ibis Gardens!' Boston puffed out his chest, waited for them to see the point.

'What is it?' Mel asked. 'This unique new experience?'

'Don't you get it? We advertise a half-day trip, setting off by bus from Ibis Gardens to Dixie Springs. We send them out in boats to see the dolphins. We get an expert like Steve or Mel to be the guide!' He spread his palms wide. 'We go one better than showing them dolphins in captivity. We show them "Dolphins in the Deep"!'

'Whose idea was it, really?' Mandy asked Jerry.

The group of rescuers stood at the quayside after Will Boston and his pilot had flown off in the helicopter to begin making firm plans for their 'Dolphins in the Deep' experience.

The sun was already sinking low in the afternoon sky. With luck, the school of dolphins would come back into the bay at dusk and they might be able to see how Bing had settled in.

Joel's grandfather grinned. 'Let's just say I

helped him to see green instead of red!'

'Will Boston's gone Green!' Mel shook his head and laughed. 'I never figured him as a friend of the earth!'

'Or of the sea,' Lauren agreed. 'But who's complaining, if it means no more dolphin shows at Ibis Gardens?'

'He plans to convert the pools into a bigger area for the alligators,' Steve told them, his arms resting on the harbour rail as he gazed out to sea. 'The biggest and the best 'gator park in Florida!'

'He never misses a chance,' Mel told them. He and Steve had agreed to help run Boston's new scheme, though they warned him they couldn't guarantee that visitors would see a spectacular ride like the one Bing had given Mandy every time they took out a boat load of tourists.

'So everyone's happy?' Jerry checked with Joel and Mandy.

They nodded.

'I guess we'll miss Bing,' Joel admitted. 'But it sure feels good to help him get his freedom.'

Mandy nodded and pointed out to sea.

In the distance a school of dolphins had broken the surface. They played and lazed in the setting sun.

'Can you see him?' Eagerly Joel scanned the horizon, hoping for proof that their dolphin had safely joined the others.

Mandy felt the warmth of the sun on her face. She shaded her eyes with both hands. 'There!' she pointed.

A shiny, sleek dolphin broke the surface apart from the main school. He leaped clear of the water in a fountain of bright water drops. He rolled as he arched through the air, flicking his tail and waving his flippers.

'It is; it's Bing!' Joel waved as the dolphin hit the water and dived down.

'I'd know him anywhere,' Mandy murmured. 'He was saying goodbye!'

And now, out there in the crystal-clear depths, Bing would learn what it meant to be free. 'It's the best feeling in the world,' she said quietly. 'It always is.'

LUCY DANIELS

Whale

— *in the* —

Waves

Illustrations by Jenny Gregory

Hodder
Children's
Books

a division of Hodder Headline Limited

Whale in the Waves

Special thanks to Sue Welford
Thanks also to C. J. Hall, B.Vet.Med., M.R.C.V.S., for reviewing
the veterinary material contained in this book.

Animal Ark is a trademark of Working Partners Limited
Text copyright © 1998 Working Partners Limited
Created by Working Partners Limited, London W6 0QT
Original series created by Ben M. Baglio
Illustrations copyright © 1998 Jenny Gregory

First published as a single volume in Great Britain in 1998
by Hodder Children's Books

One

'Look, Mandy, there's Abersyn!' Mandy Hope's best friend, James Hunter, pointed excitedly. His dad's car had just driven over the crest of a hill and the Welsh fishing village where James and Mandy were to stay for the half-term week's holiday came into view.

'Ooh, it looks brilliant!' Mandy exclaimed. She felt a tight knot of expectation in her stomach. The village *did* look brilliant . . . white cottages gleaming in the sun, the sea bordering a curving stretch of golden sand.

Moored in the harbour the other side of the

breakwater was a fleet of brightly-painted fishing boats. Against the blue sky, they looked like something out of a picture postcard.

Beside her, James craned his neck. Then he pointed again. 'Hey, look! You can just see my cousin's house!'

James's cousin, Jenny, lived with her parents in a white fisherman's cottage set just back from the road that ran parallel with the sea wall. When James's uncle and aunt had invited him to spend a week's holiday there, they had asked if Mandy would like to come too. Mandy, James and Mr Hunter had left the Yorkshire village of Welford early that morning. James's dad had taken a day off to drive them there. He was staying for lunch, then returning home that afternoon.

'What a lovely place to live,' Mandy breathed. She loved Welford, but to live so close to the sea must be wonderful too. Mandy's parents, Adam and Emily Hope, were Welford's vets and ran a busy surgery called Animal Ark. Mandy loved all animals and wanted to be a vet herself one day. She just couldn't wait to meet Jenny and her mongrel dog, Muffin. James had already told her Muffin was full of mischief, like his dog, Blackie, who was back home in Welford.

As they drove down the hill, James pointed out one of the fishing boats in the harbour. 'That blue one could be Ivor's,' he said. 'Jenny told me he'd given it a new coat of blue paint.'

'Who's Ivor?' Mr Hunter asked from the driver's seat.

'You remember, Dad,' James answered. 'Uncle Thomas's friend, Ivor Evans.' James's uncle was his dad's brother. 'We met him when we came here before. He took me and Jenny out for a trip in his boat.'

Mr Hunter shifted around in his seat, stiff from the long journey from Yorkshire. 'Oh, yes. Tall chap with red hair. He was only a teenager then. I remember thinking he was a bit young to have a fishing boat all of his own.'

James grinned. 'He told me he'd had a boat since he was ten.'

'Lucky thing,' Mandy said. Her feeling of excitement grew and grew as the car headed down towards the village. The village was set in a natural harbour shaped like a horseshoe. On its northern curve was the village. The southern side was steeper with rocks running down to the sea.

A small terrace of houses, a little cafe, a village store and a fish and chip shop flanked the seafront road.

On either side of the harbour, waves surged against rugged outcrops of rock. Seagulls circled, and beyond, the Atlantic Ocean stretched, blue and shimmering, out to the horizon. Mandy could hardly tear her eyes away.

Then suddenly she spotted something that made her gasp with surprise. She clutched James's sleeve. 'Hey, James, look!'

'What?'

'There!' As Mandy spoke, a silvery spray of water jetted from the surface of the sea. A huge humped back broke through the waves, then another . . . then a smaller one close behind.

Mandy could hardly believe her eyes. Three whales were swimming out in the deep water! It was almost as if they had come to welcome her.

Beside her, James drew in his breath. 'Wow! Whales!'

'Don't be silly,' Mr Hunter said from the

front seat. 'You're imagining things.'

'No, we're not, honestly,' Mandy said quickly. 'Look.'

But when Mr Hunter pulled in to the side of the road and looked, the water was smooth and flat again. The whales had disappeared beneath the surface.

'They *were* there, Dad,' James insisted. 'I saw them too.'

Mr Hunter grinned and shook his head. 'Wishful thinking, you two,' he said. 'You'll have to be content with Welsh sheep and Welsh ponies this holiday. There's bound to be plenty of both.'

Mandy's heart pounded. It didn't matter what Mr Hunter said. There *were* whales out there. She and James had definitely seen them.

All the way down the hill she kept her eye on the sea. But now there was only a fishing vessel chugging out from the harbour. Maybe the whales had just been swimming by and she would never see them again.

By now they had reached the bottom of the hill and James was waving madly at a dark-haired girl with a ponytail who was standing at the top of a flight of stone steps. She had a round face and dark, sparkling eyes, and was holding a small, scruffy, honey-coloured dog on a lead. She was gazing anxiously up the road.

'There's Jenny!' James wound down the window and yelled. 'Hey, Jenny, we're here!'

A grin spread across Jenny's face as she waved back. She picked up the little dog and waggled his paw at them. Mandy laughed and waved too. James had told her the dog's name – Muffin – was short for 'Ragamuffin', and now she could see why he had been called that.

Jenny put the dog down and began running along the top of the wall. She jumped down just as the car stopped outside the house. She opened the door and put her head inside. 'Hi! We thought you'd never get here.'

Jenny spoke with a soft Welsh accent. Muffin was jumping up and barking excitedly. 'Meet Muffin,' she said, grinning. 'He's heard all about you.'

Later, when Mandy had been introduced to Jenny's mum – James's Auntie Gwyn – and they'd all had lunch, Jenny took them upstairs to unpack their things. Jenny's dad, Thomas, was a coast

warden and was out on patrol. He would be back later.

Mandy was going to share Jenny's bedroom. It was a sunny room that overlooked the sea. *How lovely it will be to lie in bed and listen to the sound of the waves breaking on the shore*, Mandy thought.

'So what sort of things do you like to do in Welford?' Jenny asked Mandy, as they unpacked her rucksack and put her things away.

'Well, I spend as much time as I can with animals,' Mandy replied. 'My mum and dad are both vets, and I want to be one too.' They had finished putting her things away now and she sat on the bed cuddling Muffin.

Jenny laughed. 'That's lucky, then.'

'Yes.' Mandy laughed too.

'My dad gets to deal with quite a lot of animals,' Jenny said. 'Wild ones, that is . . . and seabirds, they're his favourite thing.'

Mandy was just about to ask her exactly what a coast warden did when James came in. He was going to sleep in a tiny room right up under the eaves of the cottage and had been upstairs unpacking his rucksack.

'Come on, you two,' he said. 'I'm dying to get down to the beach.'

Downstairs, James's dad was just off.

'Give Blackie a hug for me, please,' James asked him as they said farewell.

'I will,' Mr Hunter said. 'And behave yourselves, you two.'

'We will,' James promised.

After waving goodbye to Mr Hunter, Mandy, James and Jenny told Auntie Gwyn they were going down to the beach. Muffin was barking excitedly at the prospect of going for a walk.

'It's his favourite thing,' Jenny explained as they crossed the road and went down the beach steps. 'He's mad about hunting in the rock pools.'

James laughed. 'What does he hunt for?'

'Anything that moves,' Jenny said. 'Shrimp, crabs, tiny fish . . . but he never catches any of them. They're too quick for him.'

They saw exactly what she meant as they ran along the beach and round the corner of the cliff to the rock pools. Mandy took deep breaths of fresh, sea air as the soft breeze brushed her face. It felt wonderful.

Muffin was way ahead, running to and fro sniffing each pool, his bushy tail waving like a flag. Once or twice he jumped in, splashing around until he was soaking wet. Then he leaped on to a tall rock and stood there waiting for them to catch up.

Mandy told Jenny about the whales. 'I *know* we saw them,' she said. 'Even though James's dad said we were imagining things.'

Jenny laughed. 'You definitely weren't imagining things,' she assured Mandy. 'I saw them too when I was hanging about waiting for you.'

She had clambered up on to the rock with Muffin and was gazing out to sea, her hands shielding her eyes from the glare of the sun. 'But I can't see them now,' she called.

'Maybe they were just swimming past,' Mandy said.

'Yes,' Jenny agreed. 'Maybe.' She jumped down. 'Come on, let's go and tell Ivor. Do you remember Dad's friend, Ivor, James? He'll be sorry if he missed the whales. He loves them.'

James nodded enthusiastically.

Jenny called Muffin but he had scrambled down and disappeared.

'That dog!' Jenny stood with her hands on her

hips. 'He *never* comes when he's called.'

Mandy and James looked at one another then burst out laughing.

'What's up?' Jenny said, her eyes still scanning the rocks for signs of Muffin.

'He reminds us of my dog, Blackie,' James said. 'He hardly ever comes when *he*'s called either.'

They eventually found Muffin at the mouth of a cave, barking and listening to the echo of his voice as it bounced back at him. Jenny scolded him and fixed on his lead.

On the way to the harbour she said, 'I'll take you to meet Ivor's mum first if you like. She runs the cafe on the seafront. Her cat, Mickey, is Muffin's best friend.'

Muffin wasn't allowed inside so they tied him up by the door and went in. The cafe was quite small, but brimming with customers. The tables were covered with bright checked cloths and napkins to match. Behind the counter, a cook was busy frying burgers and chips. Mrs Evans was serving people with their meals. She had blonde hair, wore bright red lipstick and chatted to the customers as she trotted to and fro.

Jenny introduced her to Mandy and James.

'James!' Mrs Evans exclaimed. 'I remember you when you were a little boy. My, how you've grown.'

James went red and shuffled his feet. 'Well, it *was* five years ago,' he mumbled.

Mandy chuckled to herself. James always got embarrassed when people said things like that.

Mrs Evans laughed. 'So it was. It would be funny if you hadn't grown then, wouldn't it? I remember when you—'

'And this is Mandy,' Jenny interrupted hastily before Mrs Evans could go on about James's previous visit. 'She's James's best friend. Her mum and dad are vets.'

'Vets? How wonderful. Do you have lots of animals of your own?' Mrs Evans asked.

Mandy shook her head. 'No, but I know lots of people with pets and I help out with them sometimes. It's almost as good.'

'That's nice, then, dear.' Mrs Evans said. 'My father kept goats . . . a real nuisance they were. They ate everything they could find. Ate my mother's best Sunday hat once. She was livid.'

Mandy laughed. 'I bet.'

Mrs Evans went on, hardly stopping to take a breath. 'We've got a cat. His name's Mickey. He's long haired, black with a white patch over his eye and one white ear. We got him from the rescue centre in Rhydfellin. He just loves Jenny's dog. I've never seen a dog and cat play like they do.'

Mandy couldn't help eyeing the ice-cream cabinet.

Mrs Evans must have seen her looking because she broke off telling them about the cat and said, 'Why don't you all help yourself to an ice cream?'

'Oh, wow, can we?' Jenny said.

Mrs Evans smiled. ' 'Course you can, dear. Don't let it spoil your tea, though. And you can take one to Ivor. If you hurry, you might just get there before it melts.'

'Thanks!' Mandy said.

'Why don't you fetch Muffin and take him round the back to see Mickey first?' Mrs Evans suggested. 'I'm sure he'll be pleased to see him.'

Mickey was asleep in a little patch of sun by the window of Mrs Evans's sitting-room. When Mandy, James and Jenny arrived with Muffin, he got up, stretched and yawned, then began rubbing himself against Muffin's face.

'Ooh, he's beautiful!' Mandy tickled Mickey behind his white ear. 'And I can see he and Muffin are great friends.'

They played with the dog and cat for a while, then got their ice creams and made their way down to the harbour.

They found Ivor mending nets on his fishing boat. The boat's name was written on the side: *Seaspray*, along with a number, RX 43, her registered fishing fleet number.

Mandy thought *Seaspray* was a great name and could just imagine the boat's sharp bow cutting through the waves as she ploughed her way to the fishing grounds.

Jenny called Ivor's name from the harbour wall and he peered over the side at them. When he saw who it was, he waved and grinned and told them to climb aboard.

Ivor was tall and lean with a face brown from the sun and red hair, just as Mr Hunter had said. He wore jeans and long wellington boots and a white T-shirt. Mandy thought he looked about the same age as Simon, the nurse at Animal Ark.

He took his ice cream gratefully as Jenny introduced Mandy and James.

'James!' Ivor said. 'I remember you. You've grown a bit.'

James raised his eyebrows. 'Yes,' he said.

When they told Ivor about the whales, his face lit up. 'I'd hoped we'd see some this year. They're such wonderful creatures,' he said.

'They came to welcome us to Wales,' Mandy said, laughing.

Suddenly, Jenny had an idea. 'Oh, Ivor, I don't suppose you could take us out so we can get a closer look, could you?'

'What, a whale-watching trip?' Ivor said. 'That sounds fun.'

Mandy drew in her breath. 'It would be lovely if you could,' she said. She had read about whale-watching trips in America and had always longed to go on one. 'I'd really love to see them close up.'

'It's a great idea.' Ivor finished his ice cream, then piled the net on the deck beside a coil of rope. 'But I think you'd better ask your parents if it's OK first, Jenny.'

'I'm sure it will be, but we'll ask anyway.' Jenny

was already halfway down the gangplank. 'Come on, you two,' she called impatiently. 'Let's go!'

Mandy felt a quick heartbeat of excitement as she and James hurried after Jenny. A real whale-watching trip! It would be absolutely fantastic.

Ivor leaned over the side. 'If your mum says it's OK, could you pop into the cafe and tell Mum I'll be late for my tea?'

Jenny waved her hand as they dashed along the quayside.

'OK,' she called. 'See you soon!'

Two

Jenny's mum was watering her pot plants in the back yard when Jenny, Mandy and James arrived. They burst through the gate and blurted out their request to go out in *Seaspray*.

'Of course you can,' she said. 'But you be careful now and do as Ivor tells you. And make sure you wear life-jackets.'

Jenny hugged her mother quickly. 'We will.' Her eyes shone. 'Thanks, Mum.'

'And look after Muffin,' her mum said. 'We don't want him falling over the side.'

'We will. Thanks, Auntie Gwyn,' James called over

his shoulder as they ran out and raced along to the cafe. They hurriedly gave Mrs Evans Ivor's message, then dashed along to the harbour.

When they ran up the gangplank Ivor was just tuning into the weather forecast on his two-way radio.

'Going to be a bit stormy this week,' he told them as they put on life-jackets. 'So this might be the only chance you get. I'm not sure you'd like it out there in heavy weather.'

Mandy stood in the bow, breathing in the fresh, salty air as *Seaspray* chugged out to sea. She didn't care *how* rough it might get; seeing whales was an opportunity she simply couldn't miss.

'Ever been on a fishing boat before?' Ivor asked her when she went into the wheelhouse to talk to him.

Mandy shook her head. 'No.'

'Take a look around then if you like,' he said.

Mandy was fascinated by the compact wheelhouse and cabin, the lockers where everything was stowed, the little stove for making hot drinks and soup when Ivor was out at sea on cold winter days.

'Do you go fishing by yourself?' Mandy asked Ivor.

He shook his head. 'I run *Seaspray* with a mate of mine,' he said. 'He's on holiday this week so I'm having to manage by myself.'

Mandy went back on deck. The fishing gear was stowed neatly along the sides and there was a winch to wind in the nets that lay in neat coils along the decks.

The wind blew a lock of Mandy's fair hair across her eyes as she gazed out to sea. Her eyes searched desperately for sight of the whales. Her heart thudded as she whispered under her breath, 'Please be here.' This would *really* be something to tell everyone when she got home. She brushed her hair back, holding her face to the breeze. The air was fresh and clear as crystal.

Jenny leaned against the rail with Muffin close to her side. She held tightly on to his lead. James had gone into wheelhouse and was examining all the dials and switches on the radio and asking Ivor details about the engine.

When they were a good distance out to sea, Ivor called out: 'Whales tend to stick to the lay of the land so we'll cruise along the coastline, see if we can spot them.'

Mandy scanned the water. Once or twice she thought she spotted something but it was only the dark greeny-blue of the waves, rising and falling in front of the bow.

Then, suddenly, Jenny gave a cry, stood up and pointed excitedly. 'There they are . . . look!'

James came out of the wheelhouse. Ivor leaned out with a pair of binoculars in his hand. He put them to his eyes. 'You're right, Jenny. It's them!'

Mandy's heart gave a great thump. She could see the whales easily without the aid of binoculars – two great, grey heads rising and falling, then another smaller one beside them.

'I think they've got a baby with them!' Jenny shouted above the noise of the engine.

'A calf,' Mandy called. 'A baby whale is called a calf.'

'Calf, then,' Jenny answered. 'I'm sure it is one. Can you see it?'

Mandy *could* see the whale calf. It was a lot smaller than the other two, only about three or four metres long. The others, at least nine metres in length, Mandy thought, swam close to it, their dark grey heads and bodies rising up and down with the swell of the ocean.

'We won't go too close,' Ivor called. 'We don't want to scare them.'

As he spoke, two great spouts of warm gas and steam jetted from the surface, then one smaller one. Mandy clutched on to the rail. Her heart was pounding. The whales had got to be the most wonderful creatures she had ever seen. They were so huge, yet so elegant in the water, it was almost unbelievable.

Beside her, James stood spellbound. He took off his glasses, rubbed the lenses on the knee of his jeans, then put them back on again, as if he couldn't really believe what he was seeing.

'Wow,' he breathed. 'Excellent!'

Ivor slowed the engine to a chug. The boat bobbed up and down like a cork. The whales were closer now, swimming then turning, their enormous fish-like tails appearing briefly above the surface before smacking the waves in a burst of white foam as they turned and headed in towards the shore.

'It's so nice here, they don't want to leave,' Mandy said.

Ivor laughed. 'I'm afraid some of the other fishermen wouldn't be very pleased about that!'

Mandy felt puzzled. Surely *everyone* thought whales were wonderful creatures. 'Why not?' she asked.

'Whales eat a lot of fish,' Ivor explained. 'They mostly feed on krill and plankton . . . you know, the really tiny sea creatures, but these smaller whales eat cod and haddock, too. And other fish – fish that we catch for our living.'

Mandy drew in her breath indignantly. 'But they're wild creatures . . . they're *entitled* to eat exactly what they like.'

'You don't have to convince *me* of that, Mandy, but you might have to convince some of the other fishermen,' Ivor said.

Mandy frowned. Surely the fishermen couldn't be so mean as to begrudge the whales a few fish!

'I will,' she said. 'Definitely. If you hear any of them complaining, just send them to me.'

Ivor laughed. 'I will, I promise.'

Ivor turned *Seaspray* in a circle, chugging back to the place where they had seen the whales. He sailed up and down for a while but it looked as if they had gone for the time being. Eventually, he turned the boat and headed back towards the harbour.

'Thanks, Ivor,' James said, as they disembarked and helped tie the mooring ropes. 'That was absolutely great.'

'No problem,' Ivor grinned.

'Come on,' Jenny said, impatient as usual. 'I'm dying to tell Mum and Dad.'

When they got back to the cottage, James's Uncle Thomas was home. His green and white van was parked at the bottom of the cottage steps. The van had COAST WARDEN written on the side and a small badge with a picture of a puffin on it.

Mandy, James and Jenny went through the back door and into the kitchen.

James's aunt took one look at their faces and guessed their trip had been successful. 'You saw them, then?' she said with a smile.

'We certainly did,' James said. 'They were fantastic, absolutely huge . . .'

'And so graceful,' Mandy said. 'I was amazed how something that size could look so elegant in the water.'

'And they've got a baby . . . a calf,' Jenny added.

Before she could say any more, Muffin suddenly barked and sat up on his hind legs.

Jenny's mum laughed. 'I'm afraid Muffin isn't at all impressed by your whale tales . . . all he can think about is his tea.'

She filled his food bowl and bent to put it beside him. She frowned. 'Pooh,' she said. 'This dog smells of fish. You'd better give him a bath after tea, love.'

Jenny pulled a face. 'Do I have to?' she said. She turned to the others. 'He loves splashing around in the sea but he hates being bathed,' she said. 'I end up getting wetter than he does.'

Mandy laughed. 'We'll help, won't we, James?'

'Certainly will,' James agreed.

Jenny's dad was sitting at the dining-room table reading the local paper and still wearing his green warden's uniform. Jenny ran in and gave him a hug. 'You'll never guess where we've been.'

'No need,' her dad said, hugging her back. 'Your mum's already told me.'

He shook hands with James and grinned at Mandy. She felt surprised. She hadn't expected him to look so much like James's dad, even though they were brothers. He had the same shock of brown hair and round face but his skin was weathered by the sun and the wind.

'Great to meet you, Mandy,' he said.

'Dad, we saw three—' Jenny began breathlessly.

Her mum interrupted. 'Tell your dad while we're having tea, love,' she said. 'Go and wash your hands, all of you.'

She set a pot of tea down in the centre of the table. There was a loaf of bread cut into thick slices, a dish of creamy butter, some cheese, scones and home-made cakes. Mandy's mouth watered. The sea air had really given her an appetite.

When they came back from washing their hands, Jenny blurted out the details of their whale-watching trip.

'They'll be Minke whales, I expect,' her dad said, after he had listened to their description.

Mandy and James looked at one another, then at Uncle Thomas.

'Minke?' Mandy repeated. 'What a lovely name. How do you spell it?'

He told her.

'It rhymes with Pinky,' she chuckled.

'Yes – and "stinky",' Auntie Gwyn said. She

frowned down at Muffin who was sitting at her feet hoping for a titbit. She pushed him gently away with her toe. 'The sooner you give this dog a bath, the better, Jenny.'

'I will, honestly,' Jenny said. She turned eagerly to her dad. 'Tell us more about the whales, Dad,' she begged.

'Well . . .' he went on. 'Minke whales are shallow water whales. That's why they sometimes come so close to the shore.'

'What are they doing here, though?' James stared at his uncle.

'They're probably on their way south to the Antarctic,' Uncle Thomas told him. 'The calves are born in the north where the water is warmer, then they come south in the spring. The youngster you saw will still be feeding on its mother's milk. You know that whales are sea mammals, of course, and that they breathe air.'

Mandy nodded. 'But I'd love to know more about them.'

'Why do they keep spouting out those jets of water?' Jenny asked.

'It's not actually water,' her dad explained. 'When

they come up to the surface to breathe, they send out the air that's already in their lungs because there's no oxygen left in it.'

'Through their blowholes,' James added.

'That's right,' Uncle Thomas said. 'It's like a big nostril.' He got up from his chair. 'I've got a book about whales that'll tell you all you want to know.' He went into the other room and came back with a large book with a picture of a killer whale on the front. He flicked through it until he came to the section on Minke whales, then handed it to Mandy. 'There you are,' he said. 'There's lots of information in there.'

'Thanks,' Mandy said. There was a picture of a whale family, two adults and a calf just like the ones they had seen out in the bay.

James peered over her shoulder. 'How big does it say they are?' he asked.

' "Mean length nine metres",' Mandy quoted, reading from the book. ' "And an average of seven tonnes".'

'Actually they're quite small compared to some other whales,' Uncle Thomas said.

James blinked at him. '*Small*? That doesn't sound

very small to me. It's as long as a double decker bus!'

'They can be a lot bigger,' Uncle Thomas told them, 'And some can be smaller. *Mean* means half-way between the biggest and the smallest.'

'I hate to interrupt.' Auntie Gwyn said, 'but the tea's going cold.'

They all laughed and Mandy put the book down. The whales were so fascinating she had almost forgotten how hungry she was.

After tea, James went to help Jenny bathe Muffin

while Mandy helped Uncle Thomas clear away the tea things.

'It must be great being a coast warden,' she said to him.

Uncle Thomas smiled at her. 'It's very interesting,' he said. 'And I get to be out in the fresh air most of the time.'

'What exactly do you do?' Mandy said. 'Jenny said you see lots of animals . . .'

Uncle Thomas grinned again. 'Quite a lot,' he said. 'Part of my job is to monitor the wildlife and report injured birds or animals if I see them. We've got a good few foxes up on the heathland and the occasional badger. We've also got rabbits and squirrels, stoats and weasels, ponies and wild goats.'

'Wild goats!' Mandy exclaimed.

'Yes,' he said. 'You should see them climbing up and down the rock face. They're amazing. Oh . . .' he added, '. . . and we've got a small colony of grey seals below Hoopers Point.'

'Seals!' Mandy exclaimed. 'I love seals, especially the babies.'

'They have got some pups,' Uncle Thomas said. 'I'll try to find time to take you to see them.'

'That would be great,' Mandy said. 'What else do you do?'

'Oh, lots of things,' Uncle Thomas told her. 'I monitor the colonies of seabirds. This area has huge amounts of them and there's a small bird sanctuary just off the coast.'

'Are there puffins?' Mandy asked, remembering the badge on the side of his van.

'Yes,' he confirmed. 'And kittiwakes, fulmars, oyster-catchers . . . loads and loads. You should hear the noise they make, especially during nesting time.'

'I bet,' Mandy laughed.

'Then I keep the Nature Conservancy Council and the Royal Society for the Protection of Birds informed about any problems that arise,' Uncle Thomas went on. 'I patrol the long coastal path to check for erosion and damage by holidaymakers—'

'Check sites of rare plants, keep an eye on the footpaths and signposts, patrol the carparks, check fences, walls and hedges . . .' Auntie Gwyn interrupted, coming in for the remaining dirty dishes. 'Report any pollution to the environment agency . . .' She laughed. 'I could go on and on.'

'Wow!' Mandy said. 'You must be really busy.'

Uncle Thomas laughed. 'I am, especially in the summer when there are a lot of holidaymakers around. I'm afraid they don't always know how to treat the countryside. But it's a great job.'

Mandy suddenly realised that she had been so busy since they'd arrived that she had forgotten to phone home. She was dying to tell Mum and Dad about the whales.

'Yes, of course, go ahead,' Jenny's mum said, when she asked permission.

Mandy dialled the number and tapped her fingers impatiently on the table as she waited for someone to answer.

It was her dad. She blurted out everything about the whales before he even had a chance to say hello.

He sounded really impressed. 'So you're having a great time already, Mandy!'

'Yes, we are,' Mandy confirmed. 'How's everyone there? Is Mum OK? And Simon and Gran and Grandad?'

'Everyone's fine,' her dad assured her.

When Mandy had sent her love to everyone at home, she put the phone down and went back into the kitchen. Jenny's parents were talking about the whales.

'I knew there was a school heading down the coast,' Thomas was telling his wife. 'Some of the fishermen won't be very pleased, that's for sure.'

Mandy bit her lip. That was two people who'd said the fishermen would be annoyed about the whales. Ivor *and* Uncle Thomas.

'Oh dear,' Auntie Gwyn said. 'I hope they don't drive them away before the youngsters get a chance to see them again. Or worse . . .'

'What do you mean . . . worse?' Mandy couldn't help interrupting. 'They won't hurt them, will they?'

Uncle Thomas and Auntie Gwyn exchanged glances.

'They might try to destroy them,' Uncle Thomas said. 'That happened a few years ago. A couple of adult Minkes got separated from their school and were eating lots of fish. I'm afraid a few of the local fishermen went out and killed them.'

Mandy's heart turned over. 'They're not allowed to do that, surely?'

Uncle Thomas shrugged. 'Not officially . . . no. Of course, *hunting* whales for meat and oil has been banned, because the huge amount of whaling almost wiped them out.'

'That's what I thought,' Mandy said.

Uncle Thomas shrugged again. 'But unfortunately, no-one's going to know if a few are disposed of whether its against the law or not.'

'Surely three whales can't eat *that* many fish,' Mandy exclaimed indignantly.

'There could be more of them,' Uncle Thomas told her. 'Minkes usually migrate in quite large schools. And a large number of whales means hundreds of tons of fish being eaten.'

'Well, we only saw three,' Mandy insisted.

Auntie Gwyn patted her shoulder gently. 'It's no good worrying about it, Mandy. We'll just have to hope they carry on down the coast before the fishermen really feel threatened.'

But Mandy couldn't help worrying.

When she got to bed that night, she lay there staring at the ceiling. Muffin was snoring gently at her feet. The moon was shining through the window. She thought about the whale family, swimming out there in the ocean. She hoped they would swim away before anyone could harm them. She knew whales talked to one another. They made sounds like singing, whistling and clicking through the ocean depths. What were they saying to each other, she wondered.

And with that thought, and the sound of waves breaking on the shore outside, she gently drifted off to sleep.

Three

The following morning, Mandy was awake first. She threw back the covers and jumped out of bed. Muffin opened one eye, looked grumpy, yawned, then went back to sleep.

All Mandy could see of Jenny was a clump of dark hair sticking out at the top of the duvet. She had stayed up late with James to watch a football match on television and was still fast asleep. Mandy tiptoed to the window and drew back the curtains.

The sea was smooth and calm. The sun's reflection made a ribbon of silver from the horizon to the shore. Further out, the waves broke gently against the rocks. She opened the window and took a deep breath of sea air. It smelled fresh and sharp with a tang of salt.

Out in the harbour something caught Mandy's attention. Something large was swimming round and round, an enormous back rising and falling with the waves. Then, suddenly, a spout of steamy air jetted and a dark grey head appeared just above the surface. She gasped. One of the whales had come right into the harbour! Her heart jumped with excitement.

Then Mandy saw that far out, beyond the harbour, the other two whales were swimming up and down. But her smile turned to a frown when she suddenly remembered stories she had read about whales getting separated from their families by swimming into estuaries and harbours and not being able to find their way out. Was this what had happened here?

Heart still thudding, Mandy noticed that the whales swimming out at sea were of a different size. So one must be the calf and the other an adult whale. Her stomach suddenly turned over with fear. Supposing the whale in the harbour was the calf's mother? Supposing it *was* stranded? Jenny's father had told them that the calf would still be dependent on its mother and feeding on her milk. If they were separated, the baby could die!

By now, Jenny was awake. Mandy turned. 'Jenny, Jenny, come and look!'

Jenny threw back the duvet and ran to stand beside her. She stared for a minute, rubbed sleep from her eyes then stared again. She turned to Mandy, eyes round with disbelief. 'Wow!'

'Do you think it'll find its way out OK?' Mandy asked anxiously.

Jenny shook her head. 'I don't know.'

'Come on,' Mandy said. 'Let's tell James.'

They ran upstairs to his room.

James was already up and staring out of his little attic room window. 'I was just about to come down and tell *you*,' he said. 'I thought I was imagining things at first.' He took off his glasses and rubbed his eyes.

'Poor thing,' Mandy said, gazing out of the window. 'It found its way into the harbour but it doesn't look as if it can find its way out again.'

They ran down to tell Jenny's parents what they had seen. Her dad was just finishing his breakfast.

When he heard about the whale he drained his mug of coffee and stood up. 'Come on,' he said. 'I've got a pair of binoculars in the van; we'll take a look through those.'

Outside, they crossed the road and stood on the sea wall. Uncle Thomas put the binoculars to his eyes. 'It looks totally lost.' He sighed, and shook his head. 'Sometimes when whales get separated from their family groups they get so confused they don't know which way to turn.'

He handed the binoculars to Mandy. 'Here, take a look.'

Through them, Mandy could see the whale's grey head clearer than ever, and the white underside of its body and head as it rose above the water. She could even see its eyes. They looked scared and anxious, just as any lost animal would be. 'Do you know if it's the male or the female?' she asked.

Uncle Thomas shook his head. 'Difficult to tell,' he replied.

James was wriggling impatiently. 'Let's have a look, Mandy.'

She gave him the glasses. 'Wow!' he said, adjusting the lenses. 'Poor thing.'

Mandy turned to Uncle Thomas. 'What will happen to it?' she asked anxiously.

'Hopefully, it'll find its way back to its family,' he said. 'We'll just have to wait and see.'

'There must be something we can do,' Jenny said, as she grabbed the binoculars from James. 'It looks really frightened.'

Her father couldn't help smiling. 'I don't know how you can tell.'

'Well, I can,' Jenny said. 'And you'd be scared too if you'd lost your family.'

Her dad smiled again. He patted Jenny's shoulder. 'Sorry, love. You're right about that. But try not to worry. We'll give it a day or two before we really start getting anxious.'

Mandy didn't want to wait a day or two. She wanted to help the whale now. 'We can't just sit by and do nothing,' she said after breakfast as they took Muffin for a walk along the shore.

Jenny kicked at the little ridges of sand left by the receding tide. 'I suppose Dad knows best,' she said. 'Anyway, he'll know what to do.'

Mandy picked up a piece of driftwood and threw it for Muffin, then went on to tell Jenny about the time they had helped with some fox cubs and had rescued a baby owl that had fallen from its nest.

'And we've saved a badger,' James said.

'Yes, but foxes and owls and badgers are a bit different from whales, aren't they?' Jenny said.

Mandy and James couldn't help agreeing.

Mandy sighed. If it was the female that was stranded, how long could the calf survive without her? How long would the other two wait before they gave up hope and set off once more on their long swim to the Antarctic? A half-starved baby would never survive *that* journey.

Tears came into her eyes. She could hardly bear to think about the calf getting weaker and weaker and perhaps eventually dying of hunger.

They left the beach and walked along the harbour road towards the fishing boats. Mandy looked thoughtful as she racked her brain for ideas to help the whale. She remembered a story she had read in a wildlife magazine. A whale had got stranded in a narrow inlet on the coast of Australia. The local people had got into their small boats and herded it out, just like a sheepdog herds sheep. Maybe that's what people could do here if the whale didn't find its way out of the harbour by itself.

She told James and Jenny what she had been thinking about.

'It's really up to my dad,' Jenny repeated. 'Honestly, he'll know what to do.'

'Yes, of course,' Mandy said. 'But we could help him organise things.'

'It'll take bags of hard work so he's bound to need someone to help,' James said enthusiastically.

As they got near the quay they could see a crowd of people there. Word must have got around about the whale. Some were sitting in their cars, others were peering through binoculars. Lots had cameras.

When they reached the harbour, *Seaspray* was moored up alongside the other fishing vessels.

'Maybe Ivor will take us to see the whale in the harbour,' James said. 'It's only a few metres out. You could almost *row* a boat out there, and the water's really calm.'

But Ivor was nowhere to be seen.

'Let's hang around until he gets back,' James suggested.

'I've got a better idea,' Jenny said. 'Let's go and look in the cafe. I bet he's there.'

Stepping carefully over the ropes and shrimp pots that lined the quayside, they made their way back along the road to Mrs Evans's cafe.

It was full. A couple of fishermen were sitting at a table by the door. They were dressed in blue overalls and wore huge, chunky wellington boots. They were discussing the whales.

'Wretched nuisance, if you ask me,' the younger man said. He had a tanned face, weathered by the sun and the wind, and long hair tied back in a ponytail. 'Where there's one family there's bound to be more, you know. A whole school probably heading this way.'

'Aye,' his companion replied. 'Not sure what we can do about it, though.'

'I've got a few ideas.' The man with the ponytail leaned closer to his companion and Mandy couldn't hear any more. But there was something about the way he had lowered his voice that made her stomach turn with fear.

Jenny must have seen her worried face. 'What's up, Mandy?'

'Those men,' she said in a low voice. Jenny turned and stared at them.

'That's Bryan Jackson and his son, Will.'

'Do you know them?' Mandy asked.

Jenny shrugged. 'I was with my dad once when we met them along the harbour. They come from up the coast. What about them?'

Mandy suddenly realised they were staring at her and Jenny. She turned away and pulled Jenny's arm. 'Tell you later,' she whispered.

A young woman with short dark hair and wearing a denim jacket and jeans was sitting on one of the stools at the counter drinking coffee. A mini voice recorder sat on the bar in front of her. The cook was behind the counter busy frying bacon and eggs.

'Is Mrs Evans around, please?' Jenny asked him.

'She's out the back. Go and find her if you like,' he said.

Mrs Evans was sitting in her front room with her cat. 'Mickey's sick,' was the first thing she said as Mandy and James came through. 'I'm really worried about him.'

Jenny had gone round to untie Muffin from the front of the cafe. When she brought him in through the back door, the dog gave a little whine when he saw Mickey looking so poorly and went to lick his nose. Then he sat down quietly at Mrs Evans's feet.

Mandy crouched down in front of Mrs Evans and began to stroke Mickey softly. 'What's wrong, then?' she murmured softly.

'He doesn't seem to be able to keep anything down,' Mrs Evans told them.

'Isn't there a vet in the village?' Mandy asked anxiously. Mickey looked really ill and could hardly lift up his head.

'There is a surgery,' Jenny answered. 'But it's only open two days a week. Abersyn isn't big enough to have a vet of its own.'

'The main surgery's in Rhydfellin,' Mrs Evans told them. 'But that's ten miles away and I can't close the cafe to take Mickey there. Especially with all these visitors who've come to look at the whale. And I haven't a clue how long Ivor's going to be.'

Mandy stood up. 'Wouldn't the vet come to see Mickey at home?'

'I've already phoned,' Mrs Evans explained. 'But she's out on a call. The receptionist said she would tell her as soon as she gets back.'

'That's good,' Mandy said. 'Let's hope it's not too long.'

Mrs Evans lifted Mickey from her lap and laid him gently in his basket. 'I'd better get back to the counter,' she said. 'Chef can't do the cooking and the serving as well.'

Mandy covered the cat up with his blanket. He miaowed softly and closed his eyes. She bit her lip. She'd got a terrible feeling there was something dreadfully wrong with Mickey. It could be so many things – flu, a stomach infection, a virus of some kind. He could even have been in a fight, or been injured by a car. You couldn't always see wounds on long-haired cats. She sighed. The sooner the vet got here, the better.

Four

'So you don't know how long Ivor's going to be,' Jenny said to Mrs Evans when they had left the cat and gone back out into the cafe. 'He's going to be really upset about Mickey.'

Mrs Evans shook her head. 'He went off early,' she said. 'He's gone to the chandlers to get something for the boat. It's on the other side of Rhydfellin. He could be gone for ages.'

The young woman with the voice recorder was still sitting at the counter. Mandy plonked herself down on the stool next to her and put her chin in her hands. 'I suppose we'll just have to wait then, won't we,' she said unhappily.

'Cheer up,' the young woman said when she saw their glum faces.

Mandy gave a sigh. 'We're really worried about Mrs Evans's cat,' she told her. '*And* the stranded whale in the harbour. Have you seen it?'

The young woman nodded. She pointed at her camera and tape recorder. 'That's why I'm here. My name's Kim – I work for the *Abersyn Herald*. I've come to do a story about the whale.'

'Oh?' Mandy said. She told Kim what they'd found out about Minke whales. 'And the trouble is,' she went on, 'if it's the calf's mother that's stranded, they could both die.'

Kim looked at her worried face. 'Oh, dear,' she said. 'But I'm sure someone will come up with some ideas to help it.'

'My dad's the coast warden,' Jenny informed her. 'He said we've got to wait a while before there's any need to get really worried. It could still manage to find its own way out.'

'But we still *are* worried,' Mandy added. 'The calf won't survive very long without its mother's milk.'

'Do you think I could interview your dad?' Kim

asked Jenny. 'I've talked to a few locals and one or two of the fishermen but I'd like to hear your dad's point of view.'

'Point of view?' James looked puzzled.

Kim took a sip of her coffee. 'Yes, some of the fishermen aren't too pleased about the whales. I heard one of them say they could stick around for ages hoping the stranded one will get back to them. I'd like to know what your dad feels about it.'

'I'm sure he'll talk to you,' Jenny said. 'He's out on patrol at the moment, but he'll be back later.'

'Great.' Kim shut her notebook. 'Well I'm off to the quay to see what the people down here have got to say. Your whale is certainly causing a stir, that's for sure. I've never seen this place so crowded!'

'It gets pretty crowded in high summer,' came a voice from behind. 'Sometimes you can't move on the beach.'

When they looked up, it was Ivor.

Jenny jumped off her stool. 'Ivor, we've been waiting for you.'

'Waiting for me?' he said. 'Why?'

'It's Mickey,' Mandy told him. 'He's really sick.'

Ivor hurried round the back of the counter with a worried frown on his face.

'Might see you later,' Kim called as she left the cafe and headed off down to the harbour.

Mandy, James and Jenny found Ivor crouched down by Mickey's basket. Mrs Evans was there too and had told him how busy the vet was.

Ivor stroked Mickey's soft head. 'There's nothing we can do until she gets here,' he said. 'Let's hope it's soon.'

They sat with the cat for a while, then Ivor said he'd got to get back to *Seaspray*. 'I really need to fix a new rope before I go out to sea again. I'll give you a ring from the harbour, Mum, to find out if the vet's been.'

'Can we walk down with you?' Mandy enquired. 'There's something we want to ask you.'

' 'Course you can.' Ivor said.

'We wanted to ask if you could take us out to see the whale again,' Jenny explained on the way. Ivor had left Abersyn early that morning and hadn't spotted the whale in the harbour before he left.

'Oh, my goodness,' he said when they pointed it out to him. 'I hope it isn't the calf's mother.'

'So do we,' Mandy said. 'And we thought as it was so close, perhaps . . . ?'

' 'Course I will,' Ivor said. 'I just need to do a few things on board the boat, but I won't be long.'

When they reached the harbour, Jenny's dad had returned from his coast patrol and was chatting to a group of sightseers. They had been watching the whale through binoculars and one had just sailed quite close to it in his small motor-launch.

Ivor went aboard *Seaspray* with the new rope he'd bought at the chandlers.

Uncle Thomas was listening to what the man was saying. Mandy's heart turned over when she heard.

'It's definitely the female,' the man was telling Uncle Thomas. 'I've seen whales off the coast of America and learned to recognise the nursing mothers.'

Mandy frowned anxiously. It *was* the mother-whale. All their worst fears had come true.

Uncle Thomas's face was grim. He thanked the man and turned to Mandy and the others. Kim had come up to them and they introduced her to him.

'I hoped you'd be able to give me some more information for my story in the paper,' Kim said.

'Sure,' Uncle Thomas said. 'What do you want to know?'

Mandy felt sad as she turned to watch the whale swimming around in the harbour. It must seem so strange. The whale was used to open seas and the freedom of the waves . . . not houses and rocks and lots of people pointing and staring. Maybe she was thinking about the crystal waters of the Antarctic. She would be missing her calf desperately. Mandy imagined she could hear the mother whale's mournful cry, echoing beneath the waves searching for her baby.

Uncle Thomas was still talking to Kim.

'And what about a rescue?' Kim asked. 'How would you go about it?'

'Well . . .' Uncle Thomas replied, 'we need to give the whale a day or two to find her own way out. But if we *did* then need to stage a rescue, the most likely method would be to herd it back out to sea with a flotilla of boats.'

'That's what I thought,' Mandy said in a louder voice than she had intended.

Uncle Thomas and Kim both gazed at her in surprise.

Mandy felt herself go red. 'It's just that I remembered reading about a whale that got stranded in Australia,' she said quickly. 'That's what *they* did to rescue it.'

'It's a bit more complicated than that, though,' Uncle Thomas went on. 'We'll also need people to make as much noise as possible so the whale is scared and desperate to get away.'

'It sounds a bit cruel,' Mandy said dubiously. She hated the thought of the whale being frightened.

Uncle Thomas looked at her. 'Yes, Mandy, it does, but it's really the only thing that will work. Sometimes you have to be cruel to be kind. No one will hurt the whale. Reuniting her with her family is the most important thing.'

'What kind of a noise do you mean?' James asked.

'Anything,' Uncle Thomas told him. 'Drums, trumpets, people shouting . . .'

'We could get saucepans to bang,' Jenny began, 'And I know someone who's got a drum, and I've got that—'

Her dad held up his hand. 'OK, Jenny. Don't let your imagination run away with you. We've got to make sure we *need* to rescue the whale before we start making definite plans.'

'OK, then,' Kim said. 'Well, thanks, Mr Hunter. Is there anything else you'd like to say?'

'Only that if we should stage a rescue we'll need a lot of help from people with small boats,' Uncle Thomas added. 'But we'll wait a day or two before we decide.'

'Right.' Kim put her recorder in her bag. 'Thanks very much.'

'When will the story be in the paper?' Jenny asked eagerly.

'Tomorrow, I hope.' Kim grinned at them all. 'Let me know if there's any more news.' She took a small card out of her bag and gave it to Uncle Thomas. 'There's my number. Give me a ring.'

He put the card into his pocket. 'I will, thanks.'

'Oh,' Kim added. 'Do you know anyone who will take me out in a boat? I'd love to get a close-up picture of the whale.'

'Here's someone,' Mandy said, as Ivor turned up.

'Do you still want to get a closer look?' he asked. 'I'm not going fishing until high tide this evening so I'm free until then.'

'Oh, yes, please,' Mandy said. 'Can Kim come too?

She wants a picture for the paper.'

'Sure,' Ivor said. He looked at Uncle Thomas. 'Would you like to come too, Tom?'

Uncle Thomas glanced at his watch. 'I've got a meeting with the Nature Conservancy Council later, but if we're quick, I'd love to.'

As soon as they were all aboard *Seaspray*, Ivor cast off and chugged out into the harbour.

The whale surfaced as they drew close.

'Wow!' Kim clicked away with her camera just as a great jet of warm gas rose with a loud hiss into the air.

Mandy leaned over the deck rail. She could see the mother whale's eyes and thought they looked wide and scared. If only she would turn and head back out to sea. She was obviously lost and miserable, dizzy with swimming round and round. Mandy felt a surge of frustration. If only they could do something now!

Uncle Thomas was in the bow with Jenny, James and Kim. Jenny held Muffin in her arms so he could see the whale too.

As they came alongside the whale, Thomas called out to Ivor. 'Not too close, Ivor, whales can be dangerous, you know. If she dives, then surfaces under the keel, she'll tip us over.'

'OK,' Ivor called. He revved the engine and sailed round in a circle.

Still staring at the great creature, Mandy longed to be able to reach out and touch her, pat her and reassure her that if she needed help they would be there for her.

Out to sea, the second adult whale and the calf were still swimming up and down. Mandy could see the rise and fall of their huge backs with the swell of the ocean. Her heart went out to them.

'We'll have you back together soon,' she murmured under her breath, even though she knew they couldn't hear.

'Have you got a good picture?' Ivor called to Kim.

Kim waved her hand. 'Great, thanks. I'll give *Seaspray* a mention in the story.'

'Right.' Ivor grinned at her, then turned the wheel and headed back towards the quay. Mandy watched the whale as she rose above the surface, then dived down, disappearing in a whirlpool of white foam. She sighed, and ran to help lower the gangplank so they could all get off.

'Thanks, Ivor.' Kim shook the fisherman's hand when they were once more on the quayside. 'That should be a great picture.' She hurried off to her car.

'That was brilliant,' James said. 'Wasn't it, Uncle Thomas?'

James's uncle looked thoughtful. 'Yes,' he said. 'But to be honest I didn't like the look of that whale.'

Mandy frowned. 'What do you mean?'

'She seemed sluggish,' he said. 'Her eyes weren't very bright. I'm afraid she's suffering.'

'Perhaps she's pining for her calf,' Mandy said.

Uncle Thomas frowned. 'Yes, possibly. I think I'll have to decide soon whether to organise a rescue or not.'

'When?' Mandy asked anxiously.

'Tomorrow, I think,' Uncle Thomas said. 'I'll make the decision tomorrow.'

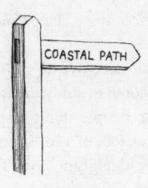

Five

Ivor went off to check how Mickey was, and Mandy, James, Jenny and Muffin walked back with Thomas to his van.

'What's your meeting with the Nature Conservancy Council about?' Mandy asked him. She hoped he wouldn't mind her being so curious.

'Well,' Uncle Thomas told her, 'part of the coast I look after is a nature reserve, and I've noticed that some damage has been done in that area.'

'Some people don't follow the country code,' Jenny piped up. 'You know, sticking to the paths, not damaging fences, not picking flowers – that kind of thing.'

'Right,' her dad said. 'We do get lots of genuine naturalists who come to study the wildlife, but I'm afraid that some people don't respect it as they should. We've got lots of rare species of flowers, and butterflies, and migrant birds. They all have to be protected.'

When Jenny's dad had gone, they decided to take Muffin for a long walk. The little dog had been jumping around and barking at everyone ever since they'd got off the boat.

'Let's take him up on to the coastal path,' Jenny suggested. 'He looks as if he's got some energy to get rid of. He's been as good as gold this morning, so he deserves a treat.'

Jenny's mum was at work in the village shop so they called in to tell her where they were going, then set off.

At the end of the High Street a stile led up a steep cliff path. They let Muffin off the lead and he scampered off, nose to the ground.

'Don't go too far,' Jenny yelled. 'He goes mad up here,' she said. 'Hunting for rabbits.'

'Does he ever catch any?' Mandy hated the thought of the little dog actually catching one.

Jenny laughed. 'Never. He's pretty fast but they're faster. They just dive down into their warren. I reckon they're just playing games with him.'

Mandy grinned. 'Thank goodness for that!'

They were at the top by now, walking a narrow path between swathes of heather and yellow gorse bushes.

Mandy lifted her face to the breeze. The air was full of the scent of the sea mingled with the dark, peaty smell of the soil and the perfume of the heather. Above, a few white cotton-wool clouds scudded across the sky. The village looked like a tiny dolls' village. The houses and the north harbour wall were shining in the sun. There was no sign of the whale in the harbour but far beyond, the other two were still swimming to and fro.

'It's great up here,' James shouted, shooting on ahead. 'A bit like our Yorkshire moors.'

He was right. If you looked inland, the landscape stretched to a horizon of dark mountains. The moorland was dotted with green and purple heather with the occasional outcrop of craggy rocks. The valley ended in a steep cliff that plunged down to the shore. The white cliff face was teeming with seabirds. Herring-gulls, cormorants, fulmars, guillemots, even a colony of puffins.

'These cliffs are called Craig-yr-Aderyn,' Jenny informed them. 'It's Welsh for *bird rock*.'

Mandy thought it was a great sounding name.

They walked on down the slope. Jenny lagged behind, waiting for Muffin to appear. 'Where can he have got to?' She called his name over and over again.

Suddenly Mandy spotted something: the reddish-brown glint of a hare. She clutched James's arm. 'Look!'

The hare was sitting in the middle of the path, long ears upright, nose twitching in the wind.

'Wow!' James breathed.

Then, suddenly, a bundle of honey-coloured fur hurtled past them. Muffin. He had appeared from nowhere.

They couldn't help laughing as the hare darted away. Its long back legs seemed to eat up the ground and Muffin didn't have a chance of catching it. But Muffin didn't seem to know that. He raced after it, disappearing into the undergrowth in no time at all.

Jenny recovered from her fit of giggles. She shook her head. 'Now he'll be gone for ever!'

'We'd better try to find him,' James said, after they had called for five minutes or more. They left the path and made their way through the clumps of thick heather until they came to some derelict stone buildings. A sign warned people to keep out.

'It's the old mine,' Jenny explained. 'The tunnels lead out under the ocean. They used to mine coal from under the sea but it's been shut for years and years.'

They were still calling Muffin when suddenly Mandy drew in her breath. 'Listen!'

They could hear barking in the distance but, strangely, the sound seemed to be coming from somewhere beneath their feet.

'Oh, no,' Jenny wailed. 'I bet he's gone down one of the shafts. Mum's going to kill me. I'm not supposed to come here.'

And, sure enough, a little further on they came across the entrance to an ancient mine shaft.

'Shh,' Jenny held her finger to her lips. Muffin's

faint bark came echoing up from below. The shaft had once been boarded up but the boards had since rotted away leaving the dangerous, gaping hole.

They lay on their stomachs and peered cautiously over the edge.

'At least he's not injured,' Mandy said. 'Or he wouldn't be making such a row.'

'Well, that's something, I suppose.' Jenny was close to tears. 'But how on earth are we going to get him up?'

'We're not,' James said matter-of-factly. 'We'll have to go and get help.'

'You two go,' Mandy said. 'I'll stay here. If I keep calling his name he'll know we haven't abandoned him.'

'OK,' Jenny said. 'We'll be as quick as we can.'

When they had gone, Mandy kept calling Muffin's name down into the shaft, listening carefully for the sound of his bark. But no sound came.

Mandy shivered in the cool breeze that had sprung up. *Please hurry, you two*, she said to herself. She wasn't sure she liked being up in this lonely spot all by herself.

There was no sight or sound of the little dog.

Once she thought she heard him but it was only the sound of the gulls squabbling on the cliff face.

Out to sea, the waves had grown bigger as the wind increased. They were breaking heavily, making white crests of foam against the rocks.

Now and then the back of the stranded Minke whale appeared in the harbour. Above, the clouds had got darker and bigger, heavy with the threat of rain. Once or twice, drops stung Mandy's face as moisture blew in on the wind.

She called into the hole again. This time, Mandy thought she heard a faint bark in reply, but she couldn't really be sure.

It seemed ages before James and Jenny got back. Ivor was with them. He had a thick coil of rope over each shoulder.

Mandy jumped up to greet them.

'Mum's still at work and Dad's out,' Jenny explained breathlessly, 'so we got Ivor. Any sign of Muffin?'

Mandy shook her head. 'I heard something but I'm really not sure it was him. The gulls are so noisy.'

'Oh . . . I do hope it was,' Jenny said.

Mandy could see she was close to tears. She put

her arm round her and gave her a hug. 'Try not to worry,' she said.

'You shouldn't have been up here in the first place, you know,' Ivor told them with a frown.

'We know,' Jenny said. 'We're sorry.'

Ivor lay on his stomach and looked over the edge of the hole. 'There's a maze of underground workings down there,' he said. 'He could be any-where.' He took a torch from his pocket. 'I'm afraid I'll never squeeze through this hole. And even if I could, you wouldn't be strong enough to pull me back up. Any volunteers?'

'I'll go,' Mandy said.

Jenny was sitting down, looking white and scared, and more upset than ever. 'I should go really because he's my dog,' she said. 'But I'm too frightened. I think I'd just go all wobbly and wouldn't be able to walk.'

'It's OK, don't worry,' James assured her. 'You stay up here and hang on to the rope with Ivor, I'll go down with Mandy.'

Jenny handed James the lead. 'Thanks, you two. I'm sorry I'm such a coward.'

Ivor gave Mandy the torch and she stuck it in the

pocket of her jeans. 'Don't go out of earshot,' he warned. 'Your parents won't thank me if we have to report *you* missing too.'

Mandy grinned, although she was feeling pretty scared. She could see by James's face that he was too.

Ivor tied the rope tightly round her waist and up underneath her arms. 'I'll lower you down slowly,' he said. 'Try not to bump against the sides.'

It seemed a long way down and Mandy let out a sigh of relief when at last her feet touched the soft ground below. She quickly undid the rope and shouted up.

'OK. Come on down, James.'

Ivor pulled up the rope and tied it round James. James was soon standing beside Mandy staring into the inky depths of the tunnel. Looking up, they saw the anxious faces of Jenny and Ivor peering over the edge.

'Remember what I said,' Ivor called. 'And be careful.'

'We will,' Mandy shouted. She clicked on the torch and shone the beam around.

'Muffin!' James called. 'Where are you?'

His voice echoed and bounced back towards them. '*Where are yoooo . . . are yooo . . . yoooo.*'

They stood holding their breath. But all they could hear was the echo of James's voice. There was no sign, or sound, of Muffin anywhere.

He had completely disappeared.

Six

Mandy and James began to make their way carefully along the dark passage. Then, suddenly, they could hear Muffin barking and whining in the distance again. But they could also hear another noise. A sound like thunder.

Mandy clutched James's arm. 'What's that?' She had a vision of a rock-fall, huge boulders tumbling down from above and trapping them.

James listened for a second or two, his head on one side. 'I think it's the sea,' he said at last.

Mandy heaved a sigh of relief. Of course, how stupid. Jenny had said they had mined coal from under the sea. James was right, it must be the ocean they could hear.

The passage seemed to stretch endlessly ahead. Just when Muffin's barks got louder they seemed to fade away again. Then, they saw daylight ahead. And something else . . . the scruffy tail of Jenny's dog, just disappearing round a corner.

They ran on, shouting his name. The passage got lighter and lighter. Then, all at once, they came out into the open air.

Mandy screwed up her eyes, blinking against the sudden brightness. James was beside her, panting.

She drew in her breath. In front of them lay the harbour, and beyond that, the village. Just above the waterline, Muffin stood on a wide overhanging ledge. The thunder they had heard was the waves breaking against the rocks.

Muffin sat down and tilted his head to one side, his ears cocked. It was as if he could see something out there but couldn't quite make out what it was.

Mandy lunged forward and grabbed him. 'Got you!' He turned in her arms and licked her face. 'You bad dog!' She tried to sound angry but was so relieved they had caught up with him at last that she just hugged and kissed him. 'Jenny will have to take you to obedience classes, won't she, James?'

But James wasn't listening. He was staring at something.

As Mandy followed his gaze she realised he was watching the Minke whale swimming only a few metres away.

'Oh, wow!' Mandy whispered.

They both held their breath as the whale came right up to the ledge, so close they could almost touch her.

Mandy gasped and her heart thudded in her chest like a drum. Muffin gave a little whine. Mandy was hugging him so tightly he could hardly breathe. 'Shh,' she managed to say. 'You'll frighten her away.'

A word from one of Thomas's books came into her mind. A word she had decided would make a brilliant name for a whale. 'Nordica,' she whispered.

'What?' James tore his eyes away and blinked at her.

Mandy explained. 'It means "comes from the north".'

'That's a good name,' James agreed.

As they watched, Nordica rose up out of the waves

and looked at them. They were so close that they could see the gleaming whiteness of her underbelly and the broad white stripe across her flippers. As she opened her enormous mouth they could see the series of springy whalebone plates that Minke whales have instead of teeth.

Her massive tail flipped and came down on the water with a loud smack. A huge wave surged towards them. It broke over the ledge, showering them with spray. It almost seemed as if Nordica was playing a game with them, although Mandy knew she was too lost and upset to be in the mood for play.

Nordica stared at her for a moment, and to Mandy, it seemed an understanding passed between them. A promise that Mandy would do everything in her power to help.

'Don't worry, Nordica,' she whispered. 'We'll help you, honestly we will.'

It seemed as if Nordica was satisfied. She whirled and dived, sending another huge wave crashing against the rocks. She swam away swiftly, then turned and came back towards them and sent a huge jet of gas up into the air. The noise was deafening.

The magical moment had passed.

Muffin began to bark.

'Muffin – shut up!' James exclaimed. He had been under Nordica's spell too.

But Muffin carried on. The sound echoed round the tunnel and seemed to be magnified ten times.

Nordica flipped her tail again then turned and sped away.

Mandy gave Muffin a gentle shake. 'You frightened her away, you monkey.'

James was still staring as the water closed over Nordica and she disappeared beneath the waves. 'Wow! Wasn't she fantastic?' he breathed.

'Absolutely,' Mandy agreed. As long as she lived she would never forget what she had seen. Nordica was so huge, yet she was so graceful in the water it seemed as if she weighed nothing at all.

At last Mandy managed to pull herself together. She knew that standing there feeling sad wouldn't do any good at all. They had to get back and ask Jenny's dad to get the rescue underway as soon as possible.

'Come on,' she said to James. 'They'll be getting worried.'

James fixed the lead to Muffin's collar and they set off back down the tunnel. Soon the daylight disappeared and Mandy clicked the torch on again.

At last they saw a shaft of daylight reaching down from above. They hurried forward and looked up to see the anxious faces of Ivor and Jenny peering down at them.

'Where on earth have you *been*?' Jenny shouted. Then she spotted Muffin. 'Oh . . . you've found him! Thank goodness! Is he OK?'

'He's fine,' Mandy shouted up. 'And we've seen Nordica.'

She saw Jenny and Ivor exchange glances.

'Seen *who*?' Jenny shouted.

'Nordica,' she answered. 'The whale. We've named her Nordica.'

It wasn't long before Ivor and Jenny had hauled all three of them up and out of the hole.

Mandy felt relieved to be out in the open air again. Breathlessly she and James told Ivor and Jenny what they had seen.

'Wow,' Jenny said, hugging Muffin. 'I wish I'd gone down after all. It would have been worth being scared.'

'I've seen that tunnel entrance when I've been on board *Seaspray*,' Ivor told them. 'I never realised it was one of the old mine workings.' He looked up at the sky. An anxious frown creased his brow. 'Come on, we'd better get back.'

By now, the clouds had gathered together and it had begun to rain. They coiled up the rope and began their trek home.

Jenny's mum had finished in the shop and was back at the cottage. Ivor went in with them to help explain what had happened.

Auntie Gwyn shook her head when they told her about their adventure. 'Jenny, you know you're not supposed to go near that place,' she scolded. 'It's really dangerous.'

'I'm sorry,' Jenny said. She had fetched a towel and was rubbing Muffin dry. 'But we couldn't just leave Muffin, could we?'

Her mum shook her head. 'No, of course not, love. But you shouldn't have been near there in the first place. You know those tunnels are dangerous. Muffin could have got lost for ever.'

'*And* they could have collapsed on top of you,' Ivor added. 'Then James and Mandy would have been lost for ever too.'

'We're really sorry,' Mandy said. 'But we're all OK and we would never have seen Nordica so close if Muffin hadn't got lost.'

'Nordica?' Auntie Gwyn said, and Mandy had to explain all over again.

'Nordica or no Nordica,' Auntie Gwyn said, shaking her head, 'you could all have got hurt.'

Then she scolded Ivor for not letting her know what was going on.

'Sorry,' he said. 'Jenny was in such a panic about Muffin I thought I'd better go with her straight away.'

Just then, the phone rang.

Jenny went into the hall to answer it. 'It's your mum, Ivor,' she said.

When Ivor came back he looked worried. 'Got to go,' he said. 'Mum's really anxious about Mickey. He's got a lot worse and the vet *still* hasn't been.'

'Can we come with you?' Mandy asked.

'Sure,' Ivor said.

When they arrived at the cafe, Mrs Evans was in her sitting-room with Mickey on her lap. His

breathing sounded difficult and he was obviously
in great pain. Ivor's mum was right, the cat *had* got
a lot sicker since the morning.

'Why on earth hasn't the vet been?' Mandy asked.

Mrs Evans shook her head tearfully. 'I phoned
again but one vet is still out on an emergency . . .
something about a horse stuck in a bog somewhere,
and the other's taking surgery. She'll be ages
yet.'

Mandy looked at Ivor. He was bending down and
stroking Mickey's head very gently. Mickey opened
one eye to look at him then closed it again.

Ivor stood up. 'We'll have to take him to
Rhydfellin. All I hope is that he can stand the
journey.'

His voice cracked, and Mandy could see he was
almost in tears at the thought of his beloved cat
being so ill. 'Have you got a basket for him?' she
asked Mrs Evans.

Ivor's mum shook her head. 'No, we've never had
to take him anywhere before. He's always been such
a healthy cat.'

'Never mind,' Mandy said. 'If we wrap him in a
blanket I'm sure he'll be OK.'

Mandy put Nordica to the back of her mind. The most important thing at the moment was to get Mickey to the vet's before it was too late.

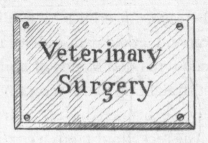

Veterinary Surgery

Seven

Before they left, Ivor quickly phoned the vet to say they were bringing Mickey into the surgery and that it was an emergency.

Mandy held the cat on her lap, stroking his soft head gently, as the car bounced along through the rain. This seemed to soothe him but she could feel he had a high temperature and his breathing was shallow. Ivor kept glancing at him now and then and Mandy could see how worried he was. James and Jenny were sitting quietly in the back seat, hardly saying a word.

The Rhydfellin surgery was in the middle of town.

Inside, there were several people with their animals, waiting to be seen. A gerbil in a small cage, two puppies, a cat and an old man with a rabbit on his lap. The scene reminded Mandy of home.

They went straight up to the reception desk with Mickey and Ivor explained that they were expected.

'Oh, yes.' The receptionist took a card from a box beside her. 'Mickey Evans. Please take a seat, I'm sure the vet won't be long.'

Just then a woman with long blonde hair, wearing a white vet's coat, came out from the surgery. It was Gillian Orpin, one of the vets. 'Is this the emergency?' she asked when she saw Mickey cradled in Mandy's arms.

'Yes,' Ivor said. 'We'd be grateful if you'd see him straight away.' He turned to the people waiting. 'Sorry,' he said with an apologetic shrug.

A young man with a puppy on his lap waved his hand. 'You go ahead,' he said. The others all nodded in agreement.

'Thanks,' Ivor said gratefully as they followed Gillian into the examining room.

Mandy laid Mickey gently on the table. 'He seems to have got a lot worse,' she said, holding his head gently while Gillian felt his stomach. The cat gave a small yowl of pain when she touched a tender spot. Then the vet looked into his eyes and took his temperature.

She stood back looking thoughtful. 'I think it's probably a blockage of some kind in his intestine,' she said. 'I'll have to X-ray him, I'm afraid. If you'd wait in the waiting-room, it won't take long.' Her assistant was already bringing over the X-ray machine.

Back in the waiting-room Mandy walked up and down impatiently. Ivor sat staring at the wall and James and Jenny sat glancing through the magazines put out for people waiting.

It seemed ages before Gillian poked her head round the door. 'Come and see,' she said, and they all hurried into the examining room.

Mickey's X-ray was clipped up in front of a glass screen with a light behind it.

'There.' Gillian pointed to a dark mass in Mickey's intestine. 'He's either swallowed a foreign object or it's a fur ball. Either way, it's got to come out.'

'Can you do it now?' Mandy asked anxiously. She had seen this kind of X-ray at Animal Ark and knew something had to be done quickly.

'Yes,' Gillian confirmed. 'Right away.'

Ivor was looking immensely relieved. 'Thanks very much.'

The vet must have seen how worried he was. 'And don't worry,' she said. 'It's not uncommon. Cats with long fur groom themselves so much they swallow fur without realising. Sometimes they manage to cough it up but Mickey obviously hasn't been able to do that.'

'He *is* very fussy about the way he looks,' Ivor said with a grin.

'I'm sorry no one could call earlier,' the vet said. 'We've been rushed off our feet today.'

'I know what it's like,' Mandy said. 'My parents are vets and their surgery's attached to our house. They're always rushed off their feet too. I want to be a vet myself one day,' she added.

Gillian smiled as she accompanied them out to Reception. 'Would you like one of the nurses to show you round?' she asked.

'Oh, yes, please!' Mandy exclaimed. 'Can James and Jenny see too?'

'Of course,' the vet replied.

'I'll wait here for you,' Ivor said.

Gillian called Jane, one of the nurses, who took Mandy, James and Jenny out to the residential unit behind the examining rooms.

There was one rabbit, two cats, two puppies and a snake in the unit. It was just like at Animal Ark, except that the room was bigger and there were three nurses there to help instead of just Simon.

'We cover a huge area,' Jane told them. 'Lots of our work is with farm animals but we deal with pets too, and we have quite a lot of injured seabirds, with there being so many of them around here.'

Seeing the animals gave Mandy a sudden pang of homesickness. There would be so much to tell everyone when she got back.

One cage held a small monkey. Mandy was enchanted. It was black with a white, hairy front and big, wide eyes. It was huddled in a corner and clutching a fluffy blanket to its chest.

'What sort of monkey is it?' James asked. He stood beside Mandy and peered at it.

'It's a white-chested capuchin monkey,' the nurse explained. 'They live mainly in Central and South America.'

Mandy stared at it. Her heart turned over with pity. She wanted to put her finger through the bars and stroke his head but knew he would be frightened if she did. Besides, she knew monkeys can give a nasty bite.

'He comes from a little private zoo just up the coast,' Jane told them. 'And he's really missing the rest of his troop.'

'Oh,' Mandy said. She didn't like the idea of the monkeys living in cages.

Jane must have seen her face. 'Don't worry,' she assured her. 'They've got a wonderful house to live in . . . bags of space. The man who looks after them is brilliant.'

'That's good.' Mandy felt quite relieved.

'What's wrong with him?' Jenny asked, staring at the monkey.

'A nasty infection,' Jane replied. 'So he has to be isolated from the others. I'm afraid he feels a bit lonely and lost.'

Mandy suddenly thought of Nordica. She was lonely and lost too. She told Jane about the whale.

'Oh, yes, I went over to the rare breeds park with Gillian yesterday to help with delivery of a calf and someone there had been down to Abersyn to see her.'

'Rare breeds park?' Mandy's ears pricked up. She had heard about such places but never visited one.

Jane explained. 'Yes, you should go there. They've got sheep and cattle, pigs, poultry . . . oh, all sorts of old breeds that would have died out years ago if it wasn't for places like that.'

'Sounds great,' James said.

'I'll just check how your cat is,' Jane said before they left. 'I would think Gillian's finished the operation by now.'

Gillian *had* finished and she came out to confirm her diagnosis. 'A fur ball,' she said. 'Mickey's going to be fine but I'd like him to stay here for a couple of days so we can keep an eye on him. I'll give you a ring when he's well enough to go home.'

'That's fine,' Ivor said and thanked her once more. 'If I'm not there my mum will take a message.'

Outside it was still raining. Ivor held his face to the wind. 'The sea's going to be really rough,' he commented. 'There's always a big swell on when we get these westerlies.'

Mandy looked anxiously at the ocean swell as they

drove home along the coastal road. Huge breakers pounded the beach and, as they rounded the corner and headed back to Abersyn, fresh torrents of rain bounced off the windscreen. A sheet of grey mist covered the breakwater. Even the trawlers moored in the harbour were bobbing up and down like corks.

As he drew up outside Jenny's house, Ivor's face was glum. 'If that whale hasn't got out on her own yet I wouldn't hold out much hope of rescuing her in the near future,' he said. 'It'll take ages for the sea to die down, and small boats won't want to venture out. You're in for a bit of a wait, I'm afraid.'

The following morning Mandy, James and Jenny were all up early.

'The whale's still there,' James said as they went downstairs for breakfast.

Mandy had already checked. 'I know,' she said.

As they reached the bottom, the newspaper came through the door. They quickly scanned the front page. News about the local MP, a picture of the Mayor of Rhydfellin opening a new swimming-pool complex, a man arrested for stealing precious birds' eggs . . . nothing about the whale.

'Oh well,' Mandy said with a sigh. 'Maybe they thought the others stories were more important, although I can't see why.'

Just then Uncle Thomas came through from the kitchen. He had been out in the rain with his binoculars, checking if Nordica was still in the harbour. Auntie Gwyn had gone off to work in the shop.

Uncle Thomas took off his jacket and boots and sat down next to Mandy. 'I think it's about time we got on with those rescue plans,' he said.

'Great!' James said.

But Uncle Thomas held up his hand. 'Now don't get too excited, James. You can see how bad the weather is. All we can do at the moment is make a list of things we need to do. The actual rescue will have to wait until the sea calms down.'

The phone rang and Jenny went to answer it. 'That was Kim,' she told them when she returned. 'She's sorry about the story. There wasn't room in the paper today. She'll try again tomorrow.'

Mandy gazed out at the rain. She could see the wind whipping crests of the waves into white foam.

Uncle Thomas had got a pad and pencil and was

writing down a few names. 'These are people I know who've got small boats and might be willing to help,' he said. 'We'll need to ring them. This evening would be best as most of them are out at work in the daytime.'

'The RSPCA have got a boat,' Jenny piped up. 'They used it to rescue a dog that got stranded on the rocks last summer.'

Her father showed her the list. 'They're already on here,' he said. He bit the end of his pen thoughtfully. 'I'll need to go and see the coastguard. He'll be able to give me an up-to-the-minute weather

forecast. Right, you three, any more suggestions?'

Jenny had one or two. A friend at school had a boat. Her teacher's husband went fishing; he might be able to help.

Mandy and James wrote down everything they could think of that would make a loud noise. Saucepans and spoons, trumpets if anyone had one, drums . . . anything people could carry.

'My football rattle,' Jenny said suddenly. 'That makes a really loud noise.'

But Mandy began to have doubts. 'Nordica is really going to be scared out of her wits,' she said.

Thomas gazed at her. 'I know, Mandy,' he said. 'I'm sorry, but we don't have any choice.'

'How will we actually do it, Uncle Thomas?' James asked. 'I mean will the boats just charge the whale so she swims away from them?'

James's uncle shook his head. 'Oh, no, it'll need a bit more organisation than that.'

He picked up his pen and drew a diagram on his note-pad: the quay wall, the rocks, then a picture of Nordica swimming in the harbour. He drew boats in a semicircle between the whale and the shore.

'There.' He showed it to James. 'If we get the boats

lined up like this, then gradually ease forward, hopefully Nordica will swim away from them, through the harbour entrance and out to sea.'

They all peered at the diagram.

'Oh, I really do hope it works,' said Jenny.

Her father put down his note-pad. 'Well, that's that. It's all we can do for now. We'll wait for a better forecast, then we can get going with those phone calls.'

'Yes,' Mandy said with a sigh. 'I just hope it won't be too long.'

'So do I,' James said gloomily.

Uncle Thomas gazed at their unhappy faces. 'Come on, you three, cheer up. It's not the end of the world.'

'It could be, for Nordica's calf, if it doesn't get back with its mother soon,' Mandy said.

'We'll just have to keep our fingers crossed,' Uncle Thomas replied. 'Look, I've got to go up to Hoopers Point. Someone's reported that part of the cliff has fallen away. Why don't you come with me? We might see those seals I was telling you about.'

Mandy's face lit up. She had been longing to go out with Jenny's dad in his van. 'Oh, yes, please.'

She turned to James and Jenny. 'Shall we?'

'You bet,' James said.

'We pass the rare breeds park on the way to Hoopers Point, don't we, Dad?' Jenny said.

'That's right,' her father confirmed. 'Why?'

Jenny explained that the vet's nurse had mentioned it.

'And we'd love to go there,' Mandy added.

Jenny's dad laughed. 'OK, if we've got time we'll call in on the way back.'

Jenny gave him a hug. 'Thanks, Dad!'

'Right.' He stood up. 'Boots and rainproof jackets, you three. And you'd better leave Muffin at home, Jenny. They don't allow dogs into the park.'

Outside, the wind was blowing a gale. It whipped their hair round their faces as they left the cottage and climbed into the van.

Uncle Thomas drove through the village and up the narrow coast road that wound steeply towards Hoopers Point. The point was a famous place for bird-watching and any rock falls might cause a hazard to ornithologists and hikers.

It took three-quarters of an hour to get there. The road wound its way past beaches, over clifftops and through small coastal villages just like Abersyn.

When they got near Hoopers Point they drew up in a carpark at the end of the clifftop road. On a notice-board there was a map with the coastal path marked, and sites where people could stop to picnic or watch the wildlife.

'We need to go on foot from here,' Uncle Thomas explained as they piled out of the van. He pointed to where a narrow path wound round the cliff edge and out of sight. The wind blew needles of rain into their faces and above, scores of seagulls wheeled and dived, squawking and squabbling in the stormy air. In places the path was very slippery. Close to the edge they could see where part of the cliff had fallen away.

'Hmm.' Uncle Thomas told them to stay on the path as he went closer, peering over at the waves pounding the foot of the cliff several hundred metres below. 'It'll need fencing off. I'll get it organised.'

They walked on up the path for fifty metres or so. In places it was very close to the cliff edge and Uncle Thomas warned them to be careful. Then they came to a place where a seat had been put for walkers to take a rest.

Uncle Thomas went closer to the edge. 'If you're careful, you three, you can see the seals from here.'

They went warily to the edge and looked over. There were a dozen or so grey seals on the beach below.

'You can only get to that beach by boat,' Uncle Thomas said. 'And it's so rocky that even then it's really dangerous.'

'That must protect the seals from being disturbed by tourists, then,' Mandy said.

'Yes,' Uncle Thomas said. 'In fact they've got no disturbances or predators at all down there, so they're a thriving colony.'

'There was a sick one once, do you remember, Dad?' Jenny said.

'I certainly do,' her father replied. 'I went round with the RSPCA chap in his boat . . . quite a dangerous operation, I can tell you.'

'What happened to the seal?' Mandy asked anxiously.

'I'm afraid it died,' Uncle Thomas said sadly. 'Some kind of virus, we thought. Luckily, none of the others seemed to get it.'

James and Jenny and her father left the cliff edge

and walked back towards the carpark. Mandy stood for a minute or two, gazing out to sea. The waves were huge, great crests of foam as far as the eye could see. There was no sign of the whales, and they were too far round the coast to get a view of Abersyn harbour to check if Nordica was still there. She sighed and turned away.

'Come on, Mandy,' Uncle Thomas called. 'Let's get under shelter before we catch pneumonia.'

'Have you got time to take us to the park?' James asked eagerly, when they had climbed back into the van.

'Oh, I should think so,' his uncle said, with a grin.

'Excellent,' James said.

The rain had stopped by now, although it was still blowing a gale and great clouds scudded across the sky. There was no sign that the weather was going to improve that day. The grey sky seemed to match Mandy's mood. She had enjoyed the trip to Hoopers Point, but she just couldn't stop worrying about Nordica and her calf.

'Have you ever been to a rare breeds park before?' Uncle Thomas asked Mandy and James when they were on their way.

They both shook their heads.

'All the animals are rare farm breeds that were threatened with extinction before the Rare Breeds Trust was set up,' Uncle Thomas explained.

'Why were they threatened?' Mandy asked.

'Oh, various reasons,' Uncle Thomas told her. 'Changes in farming methods for instance. The invention of machinery to do a lot of the work.'

Mandy leaned forward. 'You mean because people started using tractors instead of horses to plough the fields?'

'Exactly,' Uncle Thomas said. 'Several breeds of shire horse died out because of that. Then there's pigs . . .'

'Oh,' Mandy said. 'I love pigs.'

'I don't,' Jenny said. 'I'm scared of them. They're so big and I've heard they bite you if you're not careful.'

'They won't hurt you,' Mandy assured her. 'You just have to keep calm and quiet and not frighten them.'

'Frighten *them*!' Jenny exclaimed. 'They frighten *me*.'

Her father carried on telling them about the rare breeds of pig kept at the park.

'They've got some Gloucester Old Spots,' he continued. 'They used to live off windfall apples in the farmers' orchards and hardly needed any other kind of food.'

'And now farmers don't let pigs live in orchards,' James piped up.

'Exactly right,' Thomas said. 'Pigs are mostly bred in intensive units . . . so nobody wanted the Old Spot any more.'

'Poor things,' Mandy murmured.

'Ah,' Thomas said, as they turned into the narrow road that led to the park, 'but you'll see some very pampered ones today.'

They soon came to a cattle grid, then a notice announcing they had arrived. There was a white board with LLYN BRENIG RARE BREEDS PARK painted on it in red letters. Underneath it said RARE BREEDS SURVIVAL TRUST and there was a logo of a cow with enormously long horns.

'I'm going to have a chat to the manager,' Jenny's dad said when they had bought their tickets and gone through the turnstile. 'Why don't you three wander round on your own? There's a woodland farm walk you can go on when you've seen the animals in the pens.'

'The manager's a friend of Dad's,' Jenny explained as her father disappeared in the direction of the door marked 'Office'.

They turned their attention to the row of stables on the other side of the spotlessly clean yard. Mandy had visited lots of farms but this was the smartest one she had ever seen.

The first animals they found were the pigs. Middle White, Large Blacks, and the Gloucester Old Spots Uncle Thomas had told them about.

Jenny hung back.

'Come on,' Mandy insisted. 'They won't hurt you, honestly.'

Jenny followed reluctantly. A park assistant was cleaning out one of the sties. She came across to talk to them when she saw them peering over the wall at the Gloucester Old Spots. There was a huge white sow with two spots on her back snuffling around in the straw.

The assistant grinned at them and leaned on her fork. 'What do you think of her, then?'

'She's great,' Mandy said. She leaned over and scratched the pig's back. 'Feel her skin, Jenny, it's really tough – and her hairs are like bristles!'

Jenny put out a wary hand and tentatively stroked the pig's back. It gave a grunt of pleasure. Jenny laughed. 'She likes it,' she said, sounding more confident.

'Pigs always love having their backs scratched,' James told her. 'It's their favourite thing.'

Jenny laughed again and scratched the pig's back this time. The pig grunted even louder.

Then, to their delight, a dozen or so piglets suddenly scampered out from the house. They snuffled and squeaked round their mother, copying her as she rooted around.

In the sty on the other side of the yard was a red Tamworth pig. The notice on the gate said that Tamworth pigs were very like the wild boar from which all native pigs were derived. The Tamworth was a rusty red colour and had a long snout and pricked up ears. Jenny wandered off to look at her while Mandy and James stayed to watched the Gloucester Old Spot feeding her piglets.

The assistant, who had told them her name was

Sue, had finished cleaning out the sty. 'I'm just going to feed the goats,' she said. 'Want to come and watch?'

'Yes, please.' Jenny had obviously had enough of the pigs. 'Come on, you two.' She skipped on ahead.

By the time Mandy and James caught up with her, she had already offered to help feed the goats.

'Aren't they great?' Jenny's eyes were shining as she held a bucket to the mouth of a greedy honey-gold goat with long hair. 'I'm not at all scared of them. This is a Gold Guernsey.' She had already read the notice on the door. 'Her name's Hetty.'

'Right,' Sue said, when all the goats were fed. 'The Exmoor pony next. Come on you three.' She went into the feed store and came out carrying a bucket brimming with pony nuts. 'Actually,' she said, 'we've got an orphan calf in the barn. Would you like to go and see her first?'

'Yes, *please*.' Mandy said eagerly.

A nearby stable was empty although there were names above the doors.

'The Exmoor's stable is round the back,' Sue said. 'She's got a sore foot at the moment so we're keeping her in.'

'Is she the only pony you've got?' James asked as they made their way towards the barn.

Sue shook her head. 'We've got two Suffolk punches as well. They're a lot bigger, of course. They're out in the paddock at the moment. You'll see them if you go on the farm walk. Did you know there are fewer Exmoor ponies in the world than there are giant pandas?'

'Wow!' Mandy said. 'I didn't know that.'

'The Rare Breeds Survival Trust has started a programme of breeding, so their numbers are increasing,' Sue said as they reached the barn door.

She put down the bucket of pony nuts and took them inside. Housed in one of the stalls was a huge white cow with long, graceful horns that curved at the end. Her name was on the stall: 'Storm'.

They stood, wide-eyed, watching warily.

'Crikey,' James said. 'She looks fierce.'

Sue grinned. 'She is a bit difficult to handle. We've been trying to get her to accept the orphan calf . . .' She opened the door of the stall next door.

Mandy drew in her breath. Standing fetlock-deep in bright yellow straw was a beautiful calf. It was pure white with a fluffy coat and jet black ears and nose. Behind her, James and Jenny stood dumbstruck.

'What breed are they?' Mandy breathed. They were the most beautiful cattle she had ever seen.

'They're called White Park,' Sue explained. 'They used to roam in the parks of some of the great stately homes . . . that's how they got their name. They were never really handled by people and they're really quite wild.'

'I wouldn't want to get near those horns.' Jenny took a step backwards.

'Storm's OK if you speak to her gently and don't make any sudden movements,' Sue told them. 'They do spook very easily.' She went in with the calf and put her arms round its neck. 'Let's see if Storm has decided to let you feed today,' she said.

'Why can't you just feed her with a bottle?' Jenny enquired.

Sue pulled a wry face. 'She won't take to one . . . we've tried everything. She was just born awkward, I reckon.'

They stood back as Sue gently persuaded the calf to go in with Storm. Mandy held her breath as the cow's great horns swung round and she gave a low moo.

'What happened to the calf's mother? And to Storm's calf?' she asked Sue. She couldn't help thinking of another calf who was without a mother. Nordica's calf . . . swimming hungry and confused way out to sea. There wouldn't be anyone out there to try to save it from starving to death. And, anyway, you couldn't bottle-feed a whale!

The cow was pawing at the straw and mooing. She obviously wasn't keen on accepting the orphan.

'They both died,' Sue explained. 'Cows are usually good at adopting other calves . . .' She tried to heave the calf closer to the cow. 'But not this one.' She sighed. 'They're a good pair, I reckon.'

'Let me help,' Mandy said suddenly. She ran out, picked up the bucket of pony nuts and brought it inside.

'Careful,' Jenny warned.

'I'll be OK,' Mandy assured her. 'She just needs something to divert her attention.' She sidled carefully round the back of the cow and rattled the bucket softly. 'Here, Storm . . . what's this?' The cow's great head swung round. Dodging the horns Mandy shoved the bucket under her nose. 'Look,' she said. 'Dinner.'

'Hey . . .' Sue began. 'They're for the . . .' But she stopped when she saw the cow gobbling up the nuts. In fact Storm liked them so much she hardly noticed the calf beginning to suckle.

'Well . . .' Sue stood back grinning as Mandy tipped the remaining pony nuts into the trough and dodged back out. 'Who'd have thought it!'

'Some cows love pony nuts,' Mandy said. 'I went to a farm once with my dad, and there was a Jersey cow there that wouldn't eat anything else.'

'Thanks, Mandy, you've made my day,' Sue said.

'You've made the calf's day too by the look of it,' Jenny laughed.

Mandy laughed but inside she wished it could be as easy to help the young whale.

Feeling suddenly downhearted again, she turned and went outside. She looked up at the black clouds and felt the rush of cool air on her face. *Please calm down*, she said to the wind and the distant sea. *We need to rescue Nordica really soon!*

Eight

By the time they had finished the farm walk, Mandy, James and Jenny were all hungry, and ready to pay a visit to the park cafe. Mandy had already spotted a sign that said FRESHLY BAKED DOUGHNUTS and her mouth watered at the thought.

Jenny's dad was waiting for them outside the office. He was talking to someone they recognised: Gillian Orpin, the vet. She had come to look at a Soay ram with an infected foot. Soay sheep were a small breed of horned sheep originating from the Outer Hebrides.

Gillian looked pleased to see them. 'I saw the

whale earlier this morning,' she told them. 'Thomas has been telling me he's hoping to organise a rescue as soon as the weather calms down.'

'Yes,' Mandy said. 'And we really hope it's soon.'

'I've got a friend with a boat,' Gillian told them. 'Let me know when you've got things organised. I'll ask him to come along.'

'Thanks,' Mandy said. 'We're going to need all the help we can get.'

'I'm starving,' James said suddenly.

His uncle grinned. 'Let's take a look in the study centre, then we'll go to the cafe and have something to eat. Will you survive that long, James?'

'I suppose so,' James said, although he didn't look too sure.

The farm was running a special exhibition about other threatened animals. As luck would have it, part of the display was about whales.

'This is the time we see migrating whales all down the coast,' Uncle Thomas explained. 'So the manager thought it would be a good time to include them in an exhibition. Lots of school parties come here to research their nature projects.'

'See this.' James had picked up an information

sheet. 'Whales can only go short distances at speed, then they get out of breath.'

'That's what made them so easy to catch,' Uncle Thomas said. 'And that's why they were hunted almost to extinction.'

Mandy was looking at a series of photos of whaling ships. She shivered at the thought of the huge creatures being hunted so mercilessly.

'Why did they hunt them so much?' Jenny asked her dad. She was staring at a picture of a whaling ship too. The enormous carcass of a sperm whale was being winched aboard.

'Lots of reasons,' her father told her. 'Meat, blubber to make oil, the bones to boil for glue . . . hardly anything on a whale carcass was wasted.'

'Poor things,' Mandy murmured. 'Well, at least they're protected now.'

'Yes,' Uncle Thomas said. 'And their numbers are increasing, thank goodness. Although some countries still hunt them.'

James was still reading his information sheet. ' "Minke whales belong to the family of whales called rorquals," ' he quoted. ' "They were too swift for the whalers until the explosive harpoon was invented." '

Mandy shuddered. 'How horrible.'

'Come on,' Uncle Thomas said when they had finished looking at the exhibits. 'Let's get something to eat.'

After three fresh donuts and a drink each, they set off for home.

Mandy sat thoughtfully in the back of the van. Uncle Thomas had been telling people they were planning to help the stranded whale but they hadn't really done anything about it yet. Making lists and diagrams was fine, but supposing the weather calmed down all of a sudden? They hadn't phoned anyone and no one would know what they were planning or how much help they needed.

She leaned forward. 'Don't you think we should start ringing people?' she said to Jenny's dad. 'If they're going to get their boats ready to come and help us they'll need a bit of notice.'

'I know,' Uncle Thomas said. 'But really, Mandy, it's still too rough. we don't want people turning up and having to go home again. It will just be wasting their time.'

'Yes,' Mandy sat back with a sigh. 'I suppose so.'

As they drove down the road towards Abersyn,

Mandy could see the white-capped waves heaving around in the harbour. There was no sign of Nordica and it seemed that even she had taken refuge beneath the surface.

'I can't see her,' James said, craning his neck. 'Maybe she's got out by herself?'

But soon after he said that Nordica's dark head appeared. Mandy sighed again. How much longer could Nordica's baby survive without her?

They stopped off at the harbour. In spite of the bad weather there was a fresh crowd of sightseers along the quay. There was a television camera crew among them.

Then Mandy spotted the fishermen, Bryan and Will Jackson, walking on the other side of the road. They crossed over and headed towards her. They were carrying a wooden box between them. On the side it said EXPLOSIVES – HANDLE WITH CARE.

Her heart lurched. She whirled round to tell James and Jenny but they were further along, talking to some of the sightseers. The Jacksons had rounded the corner and were making their way along the quayside to where their fishing smack was moored. Their boat was called *Sea Jewel* and was painted black and white with their registered number on the side of the wheelhouse.

Mandy frowned. What on earth was in that box they were carrying? Surely it couldn't be dynamite? It would be far too dangerous to cart that through a crowd of people. But what else could it be? And more to the point, what were they going to do with it?

As Mandy took a step forward she bumped into one of the television crew.

'Sorry,' Mandy said hastily.

'That's OK,' the man said. 'What's the rush, young lady?'

Mandy didn't think she could spend time explaining. 'Oh . . . nothing,' she said.

'Have you seen the whale?' the man enquired.

'Yes, isn't she gorgeous?' Mandy said.

The television man grinned. 'Well, I don't know about gorgeous exactly, but she certainly is a magnificent creature.' He gazed down at her. He was very tall and fair-haired, and reminded Mandy of Simon.

'Are you making a film about her?' Mandy asked.

'We're from the news team,' the man explained. 'The story's creating quite a stir.'

By now, James and Jenny had arrived. 'My dad's the coast warden,' Jenny told him. 'He's planning a rescue attempt as soon as it gets a bit calmer.'

'And we're going to help,' James said. 'If you've got a boat you could come.'

'A boat?' the man laughed. 'Not likely. But it will make a good story.' He looked around. 'Is your dad here, young lady? I'd like to have a word with him.'

'He's over there.' Jenny pointed to where her dad was talking to someone.

Mandy looked thoughtful. 'Is the story really getting a lot of interest?' she asked.

'It sure is,' the TV man confirmed.

'So lots of people will be watching it on the news?'

The man nodded. 'You bet.'

'You know,' Mandy said, still looking thoughtful, 'we'll need lots of people to help with the rescue.'

'Yes,' James said. 'As many as possible.' He went on to tell the man exactly what they planned to do.

'And,' Mandy interrupted when James drew a breath, 'maybe you could mention it on the news?

Tell people we need help and ask them to contact Thomas Hunter . . .'

'Our phone number is—' Jenny began.

The man held up his hand and laughed. 'OK, OK, you're getting a bit carried away.'

'No, we're not,' Mandy said indignantly. 'It's very important. Please . . . could you?'

The man looked thoughtful. 'OK,' he said after a long pause. 'Hang on here, you three. Don't move, OK?'

He came back with his camera and a young woman with a clipboard. 'My name's Mark,' he said. 'And this is Julie, my producer. She thinks it's a good idea.'

'Great!' Mandy said. 'Thanks very much.'

'But it would be better if you explained things yourselves,' Julie said.

Mark set his camera up in front of them.

Jenny backed away. 'I'm not going on TV,' she said quickly. 'I wouldn't know what to say.'

'Neither would I,' James said. He turned to Mandy. 'You do it, Mandy. You're good at that kind of thing.'

Mandy was getting cold feet. 'Don't you think we should ask Uncle Thomas first?' Talking in front of a television camera was a bit daunting to say the least.

'Ask me what?' Uncle Thomas had spotted what was going on and had come up behind them.

Mark and Julie explained. '. . . And an appeal from someone like Mandy would go down well,' Mark ended.

'That's a great idea,' Uncle Thomas said. 'And I've just been talking to the coastguard. The weather forecast is much better and with a bit of luck we might be able to attempt a rescue some time tomorrow.'

'Tomorrow!' Mandy threw her arms round Uncle Thomas and hugged him. 'That's brilliant!'

'We need an appeal right away,' Uncle Thomas said with a grin. 'So you'd better go ahead, Mandy.'

Mark had his hand poised on the button of his camera and the sound engineer was hovering round with a huge microphone covered in a kind of furry material.

James gave Mandy a little shove. 'Go *on*, Mandy!' he said impatiently. 'Before they get fed up with waiting.'

So Mandy took a deep breath, swallowed, and made her appeal. She remembered what she had learned about the millions of whales that had been hunted and killed and reminded the viewers how precious threatened wildlife is.

'The Minke whale and her family are visitors to our shores,' she said. She smiled into the camera, suddenly finding courage she didn't know she had. 'We should do everything we can to keep them safe. So if you can help with the rescue, please ring the coast warden.' She went on to give Uncle Thomas's phone number.

A little crowd had gathered round and when she had finished they all clapped. Mandy stepped back, red in the face.

Jenny gave her a hug and James gave her a huge pat on the back. 'That was brilliant, Mandy,' they both said at once.

The camera panned round to the water just as Nordica sent up a great jet of spray into the air. Everyone laughed and clapped again. *They* might have thought it was funny but Mandy felt it was Nordica's way of saying thanks.

Mandy's legs felt like jelly. Being in front of a television camera had been even more scary than she had imagined. She sat down suddenly on one of the wooden boxes piled up along the quay. Wait until she told Mum and Dad about this!

When they got back to the cottage, Uncle Thomas said he would start ringing some of the people on their list that evening.

They had just finished tea when the phone rang.

'It's your mum, Mandy,' Auntie Gwyn said. 'She sounds really excited about something.'

Mandy frowned. What on earth had happened?

'Mandy!' Mrs Hope sounded out of breath. 'We've just seen you on TV! Me, Gran and Grandad and your dad. We were all watching the news after tea and suddenly there you were! You're a star, Mandy!'

Mandy felt shocked. She had no idea Mark and Julie had come from *national* television. She'd imagined the programme would only be seen in Wales.

The phone was busy all evening. Gran and Grandad called to congratulate Mandy. Then James's mum and dad. Then, between their phone calls to people on Uncle Thomas's list, offers of help came flooding in. What time should people come? What should they bring? When would the coast warden know definitely if the rescue could go ahead or not? They took everyone's phone number and promised to ring as soon as they knew.

Mandy's heart was singing as she and Jenny climbed the stairs to bed. All those offers of help . . . all those people anxious for Nordica to be saved. She had a great feeling everything was going to be OK after all.

Before they got into their pyjamas they looked out of the window. The moon was full and bright. Its beams turned the sea to silver. The whale was swimming slowly round and round in the harbour. Further out the rest of Nordica's family was nowhere to be seen.

Mandy's happy mood suddenly seemed to evaporate. 'Supposing they've gone,' she wailed to Jenny. 'Then what will happen to the calf?'

Jenny looked glum. 'I don't know. We'll just have to keep our fingers crossed, Mandy.'

Mandy found it hard to get to sleep. Muffin was curled up at the end of the bed and Jenny had dozed off hours ago. She heard the church clock strike eleven, then twelve, then one o'clock. The wind roared round the eaves of the house. Down the street, the cafe sign squeaked to and fro and the ringing sound of the fishing boat masts clanked and tinkled across the harbour. Mandy turned over with a sigh. It was no good, the weather forecast was wrong. It wasn't calming down at all.

And then she remembered something. The Jacksons and that box they had been carrying. In the excitement of the television appearance and the phone calls she had forgotten all about them. Supposing they had already been out to sea and scared off the other whales?

Nine

Next morning, Jenny's father got up early and went out to check on the state of the sea.

When he came back indoors for breakfast his face looked glum. 'I've been to the coastguard station,' he told them. 'The weather forecast wasn't very accurate and, worse still, we've got the highest spring tide for years.'

'What does that mean?' Mandy asked anxiously. She had already seen that the sea was still rough.

'I'm afraid it means that your whale is in great danger of being washed ashore. If that happens . . .' He broke off when he saw her horrified face. 'I'm sorry . . . but it could well be the end of her.'

Mandy's hand flew to her mouth. 'But I've seen whales being rescued from the beach on the news.' She had been helping Jenny's mum lay the breakfast table but now she stopped, frozen with horror at the thought. 'They keep them alive until the tide comes up again and they're able to swim away.'

'I remember that too,' James came in from the kitchen with a plate of warm toast. 'There was a whole school of them stranded on the sand.'

'They were pilot whales,' Uncle Thomas told them. 'They're not really whales at all, more large dolphins.'

'Oh,' James said. 'But they did get rescued.'

'Yes.' Uncle Thomas sat down and helped himself to a piece of toast. 'But they only grow to about six metres in length . . . much smaller than Nordica. If she got beached, her massive bulk couldn't support her internal organs out of water.' He glanced at Mandy and Jenny. 'I'm sorry . . .'

It was all Mandy could do to stop herself bursting into tears. The thought of Nordica dying on the beach was almost too much to bear.

'Then it could be the end of her calf too,' she

said, staring mournfully out of the window.

Uncle Thomas shrugged. 'It might survive . . . it really depends upon how old it is. I'm afraid we'll probably never know.'

Mandy felt like crying. She didn't think she could bear it if Nordica came to such a terrible end.

'Try to look on the bright side,' James said to her. He turned to his uncle. 'If she doesn't get washed up, Uncle Thomas, is it likely we'll be able to rescue her today?'

Thomas shook his head. 'I'm really not sure, James. We'll just have to wait and see.'

Along the harbour road, the quay was empty. The fishing fleet had braved the weather and had sailed out to the deep Atlantic waters beyond the horizon. Mandy had spotted them earlier when she first woke up. The bright colours of their paintwork were lost in a haze of spray as they ploughed through the waves, their hulls rising and falling alarmingly.

Down on the beach, huge waves were breaking on the shore, flinging up a fountain of white spray. The surf was riding so high it raced up the sand almost to the sea wall. Nordica was swimming dangerously close to the shallow water. Once or twice she was buffeted so hard she was almost rolled right over.

Mandy hated the thought of breaking her promise . . . but at the moment there seemed absolutely nothing more she could do.

'Well at least the story's in the paper this morning.' Auntie Gwyn came in with the *Abersyn Herald* in her hand.

Jenny took it from her. Nordica's story was on the front page. Kim had obviously heard about the rescue attempt and had added an appeal for help at the bottom.

'That's great,' Mandy said. 'But it won't do any good if Nordica gets washed up on the beach before we can rescue her.'

James sighed. 'That's true.'

Mandy, James and Jenny helped clear the breakfast things, then decided they would go down to the shore. There were spots of rain in the wind and the people who had come to watch Nordica were sitting huddled in their cars. One or two had small boats on trailers but they were left firmly in place.

Halfway down the road they met Ivor.

'Why haven't you gone out fishing?' Jenny asked.

'I'm going to collect Mickey from the vet,' he explained. 'He's doing really well, and they said I can fetch him home.' He gazed at Mandy. 'I saw you on TV last night, Mandy. You're a star.'

Mandy blushed. 'Thanks. I was really nervous.'

Jenny told him about Nordica and the dangers of the high tide.

'I know,' Ivor said. 'I was afraid something like that might happen.'

They said goodbye and headed for the beach. The air was tangy with salt spray. Nordica was swimming only a few hundred metres out.

They walked along the sand, jumping back now and then to avoid the surf.

Suddenly, James stopped and pointed, his eyes wide with concern. 'Hey, look, she's being washed in!'

Horrified, they stood watching. They felt helpless as the waves brought Nordica closer and closer to the shore.

Mandy clutched Jenny's sleeve. 'She needs us to help her,' she said. 'Look at her eyes.'

Jenny was shaking her head. 'She's getting weaker. Look, she can hardly control her movements.'

It was true, the whale seemed to be rolling to one side as she fought against the waves. Nordica was having a battle with the sea. And the sea was winning.

Suddenly Mandy couldn't bear to just stand there and do nothing. She began to jump up and down and shout and wave her arms in the air. 'Go back!' she yelled. 'Go back, Nordica!'

The others joined in. Muffin too, barking louder than ever and scampering bravely up and down the edge of the waves. James ran across to the rocks and grabbed two huge pebbles. He flung them into the water. The others followed suit, yelling and running and throwing. Mandy hated frightening Nordica but she knew it was the only thing to do. The whale didn't understand the dangers of being washed up on the sand.

Then, at last, Nordica's fight with the sea turned into a victory. With a powerful flip of her tail she managed to turn and plough her way back out towards deeper water.

'Thank goodness!' James panted. He bent over with his hands on his knees to get his breath back.

They sat on the sea wall until Nordica disappeared

under the waves. They were all shivering with cold. Their trainers and the legs of their jeans were covered in soggy sand. But it had been worth it. Nordica was away from the shallows and safe for the time being.

'That's exactly the kind of noise we've got to make when we go out in the boat,' James said. 'I *know* it'll work.'

'I hope you're right,' Jenny said.

Suddenly, Mandy felt warmth on her face. She looked up to see that the clouds had cleared and blue sky was peeping out. She realised the wind had died down. She got to her feet. 'Come on, you three, let's get back.'

As they ran back along the beach Mandy suddenly felt her heart soar with hope. The weather *was* clearing up. They would be able to rescue Nordica later that day after all!

Indoors, Jenny's dad was on the phone. As they took off their wet, sand-clogged trainers in the hallway, Mandy could hear him talking.

'Yes,' he said. 'Halfpast six. It should calm down as the tide goes out. Thanks very much.'

Mandy put her head round the door. She couldn't

help her pulse racing with excitement. 'Will it really be all right by then?'

Uncle Thomas turned with a grin. 'Yes, I'm pretty sure it will. Six-thirty. Low tide and the sea should be calm. Then it'll be all systems go!'

'What can we do to help?' she asked, her stomach turning over with anticipation.

'Well,' Uncle Thomas said, 'there's a lot of people I haven't been able to contact. Lots of those people who phoned last night and left their numbers are out at work.'

'Oh dear,' Mandy said. James and Jenny had come in to listen too.

'But I've left several messages on answerphones,' Uncle Thomas told them. He glanced at his watch. 'I've got to go and have a word with the coastguard now. Maybe you three could phone a few more people and see if you have any luck.'

'Of course we will, Dad.' Jenny picked up the list of names. A dozen or so were already crossed off.

After they had all changed out of their wet jeans, they took turns in phoning.

One or two people were at home and promised

to come. Others were out so they left messages where they could.

When they got to the end of the list James sat back with a sigh. 'We'll just have to hope that they get the messages in time,' he said. 'Come on, let's go down to the harbour and see if anyone has turned up there yet.'

They put on their coats and made their way along to the harbour.

Ivor was there already, talking to a man with a small dinghy on a trailer. He had collected Mickey from the vet's and taken him home.

'Is Mickey OK?' Mandy asked, when Ivor came across to speak to them.

'He's fine,' Ivor said. 'Glad to be home, I think.'

'That's good,' Jenny said. 'We'll go and see him when we've got time.'

They told Ivor about the rescue.

His eyes lit up. 'Six-thirty! That's great,' he said. 'Hey, you three, would you like to come with me in *Seaspray*? I've already told your dad I'll help, Jenny.'

'That would be excellent,' James said. 'Thanks, Ivor.'

'You'd better make sure it's OK with your mum and dad,' Ivor said to Jenny.

'Dad will be down here soon,' Jenny told him. 'We'll ask him then.'

They went to tell the people with boats that Thomas would be along later to give instructions.

Mandy felt a heartbeat of excitement as she saw that several people had come armed with saucepans and spoons. One had a trumpet in the back of the car, another an old-fashioned brass car horn with a rubber bulb at the end. Mandy guessed it would make a loud honking noise and would be just the thing to help guide Nordica out to sea.

After that they wandered along the quay. James and Jenny had walked on ahead with Ivor, when Mandy suddenly spotted the Jacksons, stacking and sorting their boxes of fish in one of the sheds. She craned her neck upwards to look at the deck of their boat, *Sea Jewel*. She could just see the box they had been carrying stowed on deck near a great coil of ropes and fishing nets. She looked up and down. No one seemed to be looking her way. Her heart suddenly beat very loudly in her chest. Maybe she could just take a look at what was in the box . . . just

in case it *had* been explosives she'd seen.

She was halfway up the gangplank when she heard a voice behind her.

'Can I help you, young lady?'

She turned swiftly. Bryan Jackson was standing at the bottom, staring up at her with a frown on his face. She knew they realised she had overheard their conversation in the cafe. What on earth was she going to say?

Then, to make matters worse, Bryan's son, Will, noticed what was going on and came and stood beside his father, staring up at her.

Mandy hoped she didn't look too guilty. She decided there were times when you couldn't avoid telling a white lie. And this was one of them. She came running back down the gangplank. 'I'm sorry,' she said. 'We're telling people about the whale rescue and I wondered if you'd be willing to help.'

She bit her lip. These men didn't even like whales. It was hardly likely they'd want to help rescue one.

'We might,' Bryan said. 'We're not sure yet.'

'Oh . . . well,' Mandy said. 'If you can help we're going out at half past six this evening,' Mandy said.

'Right,' Will said.

She stood back as they mounted the gangplank. When they got to the top, Bryan bent and picked up the mystery box and took it into the wheelhouse.

Mandy felt annoyed. She had lost the only chance she might get to find out what was inside.

Will untied the mooring ropes and climbed aboard, *Sea Jewel's* engine gunned as he coiled them on deck. Then the boat chugged backwards away from the harbour wall, turned and carved its way through the waves and out to sea. Mandy frowned. Surely they weren't going out fishing again? They usually only went out once a day. Maybe they were going to try to scare off the other two whales.

She turned away sadly. If that's what they were up to there was really nothing she could do about it. She hated feeling so helpless.

Later, Uncle Thomas turned up with a message from Gillian Orpin, the vet from Rhydfellin.

'She's coming with a friend's boat,' he told them. 'So she said she'll see you later.'

'That's great,' James said.

'Yes,' his uncle replied. 'And we'll just have to keep our fingers crossed that lots of other people do the same.'

Mandy thought she had spent the last two days keeping her fingers crossed. But Uncle Thomas was right. That was really all they could do.

Ten

Mandy was deep in thought as they made their way along to the cafe to see Mickey. If the messages didn't get through to the volunteers in time, they could be left with only a few small boats to try to herd Nordica out. It just wouldn't be enough. In fact it might be dangerous: the whale might get confused and head the wrong way. There *had* to be a way of making sure people knew about the rescue before half past six.

They reached the cafe, tied Muffin up outside, and went in. Mrs Evans was pleased to see them.

'Have you come to see Mickey?' she asked from

behind the counter. 'Go through, he's in his basket.'

In Mrs Evans's sitting room the radio was on. A man was giving a traffic report. Mickey was lying in his basket. He had a bald patch and a scar where the operation had taken place, but apart from that he looked fine. He purred softly as they all bent to stroke him.

The word 'Abersyn' on the radio made Mandy suddenly prick up her ears. The traffic report was focused on that area. Something about roadworks and traffic delays on the road between one of the big towns and the village. It must be local radio.

Local radio! She suddenly had an idea. If they could broadcast the news on the radio that the whale rescue was to take place at six-thirty, people might hear it in their cars on the way home from work.

'Hey,' she said to James and Jenny. 'I've just had a brilliant idea!' She explained quickly.

'I'll ask Mrs Evans if we can use her phone,' Jenny said, dashing out.

James had spotted a phone directory and was busy looking up the number.

Jenny was back within seconds. 'She said it's fine.'

James quickly found the number. 'You do it, Mandy,' he said.

Mandy was put through to the news desk. The news editor listened carefully.

'Right,' he said, when Mandy had explained. 'We broadcast news on the hour, every hour, so that's three times we can give out the appeal before six-thirty.'

'Oh, thank you so much,' Mandy said.

'And we'll send someone down to report the story,' the news editor told her.

'That's great,' Mandy said. 'Thanks again.' Her eyes were shining as she put down the phone. 'Well,' she said. 'That's it. Now all we can do is wait.'

'Nordica is really going to be famous,' Jenny said. 'TV, newspaper and now local radio!'

James chuckled. 'She's going to be the most famous whale in Wales.'

They said goodbye to Mrs Evans and Mickey and went back to the harbour. Several people were standing at the railings with binoculars. They weren't looking at Nordica but had their field glasses trained on something further out to sea.

Mandy, James and Jenny stopped to stare out across the water.

'Here,' a woman said, handing her binoculars to Mandy. 'Take a look.'

Mandy adjusted the binoculars then drew in her breath. 'Wow!'

'What is it?' James said, fidgeting impatiently beside her.

'A school of whales,' the woman told him. 'There must be about fifty of them.'

Mandy was still staring through the glasses. The woman was right. There must be fifty at least. She could see their great backs rising and falling with the ocean swell. Now and then jets of steamy gas rose into the air and fell like misty rain back to the surface.

Mandy scanned the whole length of the school, anxiously searching for a smaller whale . . . Nordica's calf. There was no sign of it. She suddenly felt scared. Supposing it had died? Supposing the wait to try to rescue Nordica had been *too* long for the young creature and it had perished? She could hardly bear to think about it.

'Look, James.' She handed the glasses to him.

There was one thing she was relieved about, however. If the Jacksons *had* gone out to scare away the whales then they certainly hadn't succeeded.

'Can you see Nordica's calf?' Jenny asked impatiently, dying to have a look herself.

James shook his head. 'No, 'fraid not.'

'Nordica's the one in the harbour,' Mandy explained, when the woman looked puzzled.

'Oh,' the woman said. 'I've brought my dinghy to help with the rescue.' She looked around. 'I hope a few more people than this turn up.'

'Yes,' Mandy replied. 'So do we.'

'She's got a calf, has she?' the woman asked.

Mandy nodded. 'We're really worried about it.'

'The others will have been looking after it, don't worry,' the woman said.

'Yes, but they won't feed it, will they?' Mandy said sadly.

The woman shook her head. 'I don't know about that. We'll just have to wait and see, won't we?'

'And we haven't got very long to wait now,' Jenny reminded her.

Mandy knew she was trying to cheer her up. But if Nordica's calf was dead it would spoil the whole thing.

They left the woman with the binoculars and went to find Ivor.

He was on *Seaspray* checking the engine. 'The TV people want to come out with us,' he told them, as they went on board. 'They're coming back at six o'clock.'

They told him about the local radio station and its promise to put out an appeal.

'That's great,' he said. 'I hope it works.'

Mandy sat down on a box and put her chin in her hands. 'If not enough boats turn up,' she said, 'then there won't be anything for the TV people to film.'

Ivor must have seen how downhearted she was. He patted her shoulder. 'It'll be OK, don't you worry.'

They went down to the shop to tell Jenny's mum about the rescue.

'Get yourselves an early tea,' she told them. 'It doesn't do you any good to go sailing on an empty stomach.'

They ran home, made a few hasty sandwiches and took them down to eat on the beach. They'd also raided the kitchen cupboards for saucepans, and spoons, and metal bowls . . . anything they could bang to make a noise with.

'My rattle!' Jenny had exclaimed suddenly. 'I almost forgot.' She rushed upstairs and came down with a wooden football rattle. She wound it round and round in the air.

Mandy and James covered their ears.

'If that doesn't scare Nordica,' James said, 'nothing will.'

On the beach they sat in the shelter of the wall and ate their peanut butter sandwiches and crisps.

They counted the boats. Three or four were already on the slipway ready to launch, although their owners just seemed to be hanging around, not quite knowing what to do.

'Dad'll be there to get things organised, don't worry,' Jenny said.

Mandy looked at her watch. Five-thirty. Her stomach turned over with excitement. 'Come on,' she said, getting to her feet. 'Let's get down to the harbour and see what's going on.'

When they got there, Ivor was talking to Bryan Jackson. The two men parted, and Bryan went aboard *Sea Jewel* and disappeared inside the wheelhouse.

Ivor came to greet them.

Mandy said close to his ear, 'What did he say?'

'What did who say?' Ivor looked puzzled.

'Mr Jackson.'

'We were just talking about the rescue. He volunteered to help,' he told her.

'Oh.' Mandy said. 'But I thought they hated the whales.'

Ivor grinned. 'They don't hate them,' he said. 'They just thought they were a nuisance. They've got some distress flares to let off in case the other noises don't do the trick.'

Distress flares. They were like rockets . . . explosives . . .

'Oh dear . . .' Mandy suddenly felt guilty. She had been jumping to the most terrible conclusions. Thank goodness she hadn't done any more snooping around their boat.

'Time to get on board,' Ivor glanced at his watch.

Muffin ran up the gangplank first. Jenny suddenly gasped and put her hand over her mouth. 'Muffin – I should have left him at home. Mum'll go mad if he smells of fish again.'

'Never mind,' Mandy said. 'You'll just have to bathe him as soon as we get back.'

They settled themselves on deck. Muffin sat with Mandy. She stroked his rough fur. Her touch seemed to calm him down and he sat quietly beside her, tongue hanging out, watching the activity down below. James was in the bow, unpacking the bag of pots and pans and laying them out ready.

'Well, Muffin,' Mandy said, giving him a hug, 'it's now or never.' She still felt worried. Half a dozen or so small boats were waiting to be launched from the slipway. Some were already in the water. There still didn't seem to be enough.

She suddenly realised someone was calling from the quay, and when she looked, the television crew were there. Ivor beckoned them aboard.

Then there was a shout from Jenny. She was standing on the other side, watching for the whales through Ivor's binoculars. 'Hey, you two . . . come and look!'

And when Mandy and James ran to her side they saw a sight Mandy knew she would never forget. A whole flotilla of boats was sailing round the headland. Large ones, small ones, some with sails, some with outboard engines . . . several pleasure cruisers gleaming white in the sun, their sharp hulls cutting through the waves like knives.

More cars with trailers had turned up along the harbour road. Some were unloading, others waiting patiently to launch their boats from the slipway. There were too many even to count.

Ten minutes later, the coastguard launch appeared, with Uncle Thomas standing in the cockpit, a loudhailer in his hand.

'Right.' Ivor shouted down to a man on the quayside to untie the ropes. 'Time to go, you three,' he shouted. 'Get ready.'

Seaspray's engine gunned and at last they were on their way.

In the bow, Mandy jumped up and down with excitement. She simply couldn't help it.

The coastguard vessel had gone from boat to boat, with Uncle Thomas shouting instructions as they went. Everyone took their craft in as close to the beach as they dared, forming a semicircle from the breakwater to the rocks – a barrier between Nordica and the shore. She *could* dive underneath the boats, but hopefully she would be too scared to come that close.

James and Jenny were standing in *Seaspray*'s bow. Jenny had Muffin in her arms. He was watching the waves with his head on one side, his ears cocked.

He suddenly began barking, just as James yelled: 'Mandy . . . here she is!'

Mandy rushed to the side. Nordica was rising up above the waves. Mandy felt James shove a saucepan and spoon into her hands. She banged it as loudly as she could, shouting and yelling at the top of her voice. That seemed to be a signal for everyone to do the same.

Mandy had never heard such a noise in all her life. Trumpets blowing, drums and saucepans banging, horns hooting, people shouting. *Poor Nordica*, she thought. *She'll be frightened out of her life*.

Nordica *was* frightened. She let out a powerful jet of steam, then dived beneath the surface. Suddenly everything went quiet. Then, to Mandy's immense relief, she appeared again, swimming not far away and heading towards the harbour entrance.

'She's going!' James yelled, as the boats slowly closed in on the whale and the noise rose to a crescendo. Closer and closer . . .

Then, to their horror, Nordica suddenly turned and dived, her huge tail hitting the water with a loud smack. Clouds of spray rose in the air and for a moment or two she couldn't be seen at all. But when the mist cleared she was there . . . swimming *towards* the flotilla of boats.

'Oh, no,' Mandy groaned. 'The other way, Nordica . . . the other way!'

Surely she wasn't going to brave the onslaught and dive underneath?

The boats closed in again, hooting, banging, booming, crashing. Mandy's heart was in her mouth. She wasn't sure it was working at all. In fact the din seemed to be confusing Nordica more than ever.

Suddenly, Muffin leaped from Jenny's arms on to the deck. Jenny flung out her hand but it was too late. Muffin had gone, leaping high over the boxes and fishing gear. He jumped up on the winch and balanced there like a circus performer, the breeze flowing through his long coat. Mandy gasped. If the ship suddenly rolled he would be tossed into the water.

Then the little dog began barking. Louder than

anyone had ever heard him bark before. Nordica looked in *Seaspray*'s direction for a second, then turned, dived, came up again and began swimming rapidly out towards the ocean.

The noise continued as the boats followed, honking and cheering until at last Nordica found the narrow inlet between the rocks. With one last farewell jet from her blowhole she joined the waiting whales.

A huge cheer rose from every boat. Everyone was jumping up and down and waving like mad. Then, for good measure, one of the Jacksons let off a couple of flares. They whizzed up into the sky with an arc of colour.

Ivor revved *Seaspray*'s engine and followed Nordica out into the deeper waters. *Sea Jewel* and a couple of the other fishing vessels were behind. They all wanted to make sure the whales had really gone.

Mandy felt tears streaming down her face. She turned to James and threw her arms round him. He wriggled, red in the face, but let her hug him just the same. Jenny ran from the other side and hugged them too.

'It was Muffin who clinched it.' Mandy wiped her face. 'He's the best dog in the world.'

Then a shout went up from the *Sea Jewel*. 'Look out, they're coming back.'

Mandy, James and Jenny turned in horror. Heading towards them were three whales. Mandy knew exactly who they were. Nordica and her mate, together with their calf. Reunited.

A strange silence seemed to settle over the waves as Nordica and the other two swam alongside *Seaspray*.

In the wheelhouse, Ivor was holding his breath. Whales *had* been known to turn boats over. And if Nordica was still in a panic after all that noise . . . ?

But Mandy knew there was no danger. Nordica and her family had come to say goodbye . . . and thank you. She leaned over the side and stretched out her arm. *Goodbye, Nordica, safe journey. I won't ever forget you.*

Nordica met her eye for a moment then, with a huge flick of her tail, turned and, with the other two following in her wake, swam back to join the others.

James was sitting down. 'Wow!' He took off his glasses, rubbed them on the knee of his jeans and put them back on again. 'Wait until we tell everyone back home about *this*!'

Mandy swallowed a great big lump that had come to her throat and couldn't say anything more at all.

'Right, everyone,' Ivor called from the wheel-house. 'Let's go home.'

When *Seaspray* was safely moored and the television crew had gone back to the studio to edit their film, Mandy, James, Jenny, Ivor and Muffin made their way down to the cafe for hot drinks and something to eat.

Mrs Evans cooked everyone a slap-up meal. Mandy and James, Jenny, Uncle Thomas and Auntie Gwyn, Gillian Orpin, and Kim from the *Herald*, who had cadged a ride in someone's boat, all sat down to eat together.

Will and Bryan Jackson turned up too. Bryan sat next to Mandy and gave her such a knowing look she really began to wonder if he could read her mind.

'Thanks for all your help,' Uncle Thomas said to Mandy, James and Jenny. 'If it wasn't for that last minute radio appeal, Nordica might still be swimming in the harbour now.'

Looking at the faces around her, Mandy knew she would never forget her holiday in Wales and all the new friends she had made. But now their adventure was over, and she felt a sudden pang of homesickness. In fact, now she thought about it, Mandy simply couldn't wait to get back to dear old Welford and tell them all about the whale in the waves!

The Website!

www.animalark.co.uk

* Visit our great new website for more information about new and forthcoming Lucy Daniels book titles.

* Discover the world of Animal Ark!

* Find out about your prize-winning competitions!

* Try fun animal puzzles!

CHECK IT OUT NOW!

GIRAFFE IN A JAM
Animal Ark in South Africa

Lucy Daniels

A family trip to South Africa means an amazing adventure for Mandy and James. They can't wait to go on safari!

Mandy, James and their friend Levina are watching giraffes at a waterhole when Mandy spots one in trouble. Its legs are splayed to drink and it doesn't seem able to right itself. If the giraffe can't get back on its feet, it will become prey to prowling lions. Levina says they must let nature take its course, but Mandy notices a young giraffe waiting alongside the injured adult. Surely they can't just leave a mother and her baby to die?

Another Hodder Children's book

HIPPO IN A HOLE
Animal Ark in South Africa

Lucy Daniels

A family trip to South Africa means an amazing adventure for Mandy and James. They can't wait to go on safari!

A violent storm causes chaos at the lodge where Mandy and James are staying. When they go outside the resort to check on the damage, they find a mother hippo in distress, standing guard over her trapped calf. The warden's attempts to rescue the baby hippo fail when their jeep gets stuck in the mud. But if they don't free the baby soon, he and his mother will die. Can Mandy help the hippos?

Another Hodder Children's book

ANIMAL ARK FAVOURITES
A short story collection

Lucy Daniels

Mandy Hope loves animals more than anything else. She knows quite a lot about them too: both her parents are vets and Mandy helps out in their surgery, Animal Ark.

Mandy and James catch up with old friends and make new ones along the way in this wonderful collection of nine Animal Ark short stories, featuring favourite animals and characters from the series in brand new adventures: Prince the pony riding to the rescue, Houdini the goat foiling a thief, Tess set for triumph in the sheepdog trials and Amber the kitten on the run once more . . .

**Look out for Lucy Daniels'
exciting new series:**

Follow Jody McGrath on her travels as her
dolphin dreams come true! Jody's whole family
are sailing around the world on a dolphin
research trip – and Jody is recording all their
exciting adventures in her Dolphin Diaries

The first title, *INTO THE BLUE*,
is available from all good bookshops.

ANIMAL ARK *by Lucy Daniels*

1	KITTENS IN THE KITCHEN	£3.99	❏
2	PONY IN THE PORCH	£3.99	❏
3	PUPPIES IN THE PANTRY	£3.99	❏
4	GOAT IN THE GARDEN	£3.99	❏
5	HEDGEHOGS IN THE HALL	£3.99	❏
6	BADGER IN THE BASEMENT	£3.99	❏
7	CUB IN THE CUPBOARD	£3.99	❏
8	PIGLET IN A PLAYPEN	£3.99	❏
9	OWL IN THE OFFICE	£3.99	❏
10	LAMB IN THE LAUNDRY	£3.99	❏
11	BUNNIES IN THE BATHROOM	£3.99	❏
12	DONKEY ON THE DOORSTEP	£3.99	❏
13	HAMSTER IN A HAMPER	£3.99	❏
14	GOOSE ON THE LOOSE	£3.99	❏
15	CALF IN THE COTTAGE	£3.99	❏
16	KOALAS IN A CRISIS	£3.99	❏
17	WOMBAT IN THE WILD	£3.99	❏
18	ROO ON THE ROCK	£3.99	❏
19	SQUIRRELS IN THE SCHOOL	£3.99	❏
20	GUINEA-PIG IN THE GARAGE	£3.99	❏
21	FAWN IN THE FOREST	£3.99	❏
22	SHETLAND IN THE SHED	£3.99	❏
23	SWAN IN THE SWIM	£3.99	❏
24	LION BY THE LAKE	£3.99	❏
25	ELEPHANTS IN THE EAST	£3.99	❏
26	MONKEYS ON THE MOUNTAIN	£3.99	❏
27	DOG AT THE DOOR	£3.99	❏
28	FOALS IN THE FIELD	£3.99	❏
29	SHEEP AT THE SHOW	£3.99	❏
30	RACOONS ON THE ROOF	£3.99	❏
31	DOLPHIN IN THE DEEP	£3.99	❏
32	BEARS IN THE BARN	£3.99	❏
33	OTTER IN THE OUTHOUSE	£3.99	❏
34	WHALE IN THE WAVES	£3.99	❏
35	HOUND AT THE HOSPITAL	£3.99	❏
36	RABBITS ON THE RUN	£3.99	❏
37	HORSE IN THE HOUSE	£3.99	❏
38	PANDA IN THE PARK	£3.99	❏
39	TIGER ON THE TRACK	£3.99	❏
40	GORILLA IN THE GLADE	£3.99	❏
41	TABBY IN THE TUB	£3.99	❏
42	CHINCHILLA UP THE CHIMNEY	£3.99	❏
43	PUPPY IN A PUDDLE	£3.99	❏
44	LEOPARD AT THE LODGE	£3.99	❏
45	GIRAFFE IN A JAM	£3.99	❏
46	HIPPO IN A HOLE	£3.99	❏
47	FOXES ON THE FARM	£3.99	❏
	SHEEPDOG IN THE SNOW	£3.99	❏
	KITTEN IN THE COLD	£3.99	❏
	FOX IN THE FROST	£3.99	❏
	HAMSTER IN THE HOLLY	£3.99	❏
	PONY IN THE POST	£3.99	❏
	PONIES AT THE POINT	£3.99	❏
	SEAL ON THE SHORE	£3.99	❏
	ANIMAL ARK FAVOURITES	£3.99	❏
	PIGS AT THE PICNIC	£3.99	❏
	DOG IN THE DUNGEON	£3.99	❏
	CAT IN THE CRYPT	£3.99	❏
	STALLION IN THE STORM	£3.99	❏
	PUP AT THE PALACE	£3.99	❏
	WILDLIFE WAYS	£9.99	❏

All Hodder Children's books are available at your local bookshop, or can be ordered direct from the publisher. Just tick the titles you would like and complete the details below. Prices and availability are subject to change without prior notice.

Please enclose a cheque or postal order made payable to *Bookpoint Ltd,* and send to: Hodder Children's Books, 39 Milton Park, Abingdon, OXON, OX14 4TD, UK. Email Address: orders@bookpoint.co.uk

If you would prefer to pay by credit card, our call centre team would be delighted to take your order by telephone. Our direct line *01235 400414* (lines open 9.00 am – 6.00 pm Monday to Saturday, 24 hour message answering service). Alternatively you can send a fax on *01235 400454.*

TITLE	FIRST NAME	SURNAME	
ADDRESS			
DAYTIME TEL:		POST CODE	

If you would prefer to pay by credit card, please complete: Please debit my Visa/Access/Diner's Card/American Express (delete as applicable) card no:

☐☐☐☐ ☐☐☐☐ ☐☐☐☐ ☐☐☐☐

Signature ....

Expiry Date: ....

If you would NOT like to receive further information on our products please tick the box. ☐